# The Star
# of
# Bethlehem

An Epic Account Surrounding
the Birth of Christ

by
Michael Macari, Jr.

TRILOGY

The Star of Bethlehem

Trilogy Christian Publishers, a Wholly Owned Subsidary of the Trinity Broadcasting Network

2442 Michelle Drive, Tustin, CA 92780

For information about special discounts for bulk purchases, please contact Trilogy Christian Publishing.

Trilogy Disclaimer: The views and content expressed in this book are those of the author and may not necessarily reflect the views and doctrine of Trilogy Christian Publishing or the Trinity Broadcasting Network.

Manufactured in the United States of America

10 9 8 7 6 5 4 3 2 1

Library of Congress Cataloging-in-Publication Data is available.

ISBN: 978-1-63769-726-9

E-ISBN: 978-1-63769-727-6

This book is joyfully dedicated to my father, whose pure wonder at God inspired his son to write the story of Christmas, held in his heart all these years.

# Table of Contents

# Prologue

Few things in this life rival Christmas and the spirit it brings.

From as far back as I can remember, the Christmas season has been the most wonderful time of the year. I loved every part of it: building wreaths, manger scenes, the music, family, and the once-a-year special foods Nonni proudly made.

But most of all, Christmas was imprinted on me by my father.

Like most immigrant families, most time was spent at home. In the Macari household in the 1960s, that meant anticipating the great movies my father and mother loved. The biblical epics—*Ben Hur*, *The Ten Commandments*, *King of Kings*, and my father's favorite, *Quo Vadis*, were on once a year. These were the days before cable, VCRs, DVR, and on-demand TV. Miss it, and you would have to wait a whole year to see it again.

My father was inspired by all things God. Simple wonderment was embodied in the great movies which brought biblical stores to life. For me, it was the music as well. Great composers like Miklos Rozsa, Ernest Gold, John Williams. The grand orchestral and scenic soundtracks were, unto themselves, masterpieces. They brought the *emotion* of the story to life.

It had always been my ambition to make the Christmas story into a major, epic motion picture. After all, I did enjoy a thirty-year career writing and producing TV and video and travelled worldwide doing it. It was the one great project I wanted to do. It never left me all these years. Neither did writing the story which became this book.

I felt I would do this to honor my father, as my way of thanking him for this great gift he shared with me.

I would do it for God, to bring hope to people whom I see as increasingly hurting around this world of late.

I would do it because it simply was there, waiting to be written down.

So, about twenty-five or thirty years ago, during my business and family life, I began to research and outline *The Star of Bethlehem*.

It was a pleasure for this writer to learn about ancient times and have the opportunity to cross-reference scripture to my very heart's content. But the file lay dormant for twenty-five years.

Then came coronavirus.

It was hard for me to believe I was feeling compelled to pick *The Star* back up. I found the folder and perused through it. *Hmm*, I thought. *God knows the world needs Christmas more than ever. Can it be done?*

And so, humbly speaking, I prayed.

"God, if this is something You want me to do at *this* time, You're going to have to show up in my life. This is meaningless without You."

And, "I ask You to bless this, to inspire me, to be there with me to write these things down and tell this story credibly. If it is there, I'll write. If it is not, I won't."

It started out slow, then more, and clearer. At times, nothing was there, so the pages went blank that day. At other times, it flowed through and became ink.

After several months, the story seemed complete, at least where the events being written about are concerned. And here you are with it in your hands.

---

It seems impossible to me that such a childhood dream could really become a reality. Could there be a reawakening of the wonderment, the joy, the familial spirit that is Christmas, in our world today?

I suppose time will tell. I hope so.

Well, we did it, Dad. *Buon Natale* to the world.

- Michael Macari

# Introduction

As was noted in the Prologue to this book, the inspiration to tell the story of Christmas began decades ago. The actual, historical story of the birth of Christ goes back over two thousand years. It is a familiar story that has been told in every nation on earth and to every people group.

There is the inspired book of the Bible, which predicts and recounts the events surrounding Israel's promised Messiah from a number of ancient writers, most writing many millennia before He ever arrived.

We have heard the stories: the virgin birth, angels, and a star announcing His coming; iconic Mary, Joseph, and Jesus; the little town of Bethlehem. Most of all, Jesus' birth in a simple manger, and the wrath of a despotic king who massacred many innocent children seeking to kill the Child.

There is no shortage of material on the Christmas story today. There are hundreds, if not thousands, of books that have been written, and millions of paintings, statues, sculptures, illustrations, and historical anecdotes about the event and the people who lived it. And much peripheral material, legend, and belief.

It is an epic story which took place in a simple place and a time of unrest, not unlike our own.

In other writings and stories, He is awaited as Messiah, Savior, vindicator, warrior King. He is depicted as a suffering servant too.

However, as you look at the birth of Jesus Christ of Nazareth (born around 3 BC; died around 30-33 AD), He is undoubtedly the central figure of the whole human race—and the *only* one who ever lived who had a *star* announce His birth.

And so begins the story of *The Star of Bethlehem*.

*The Star* endeavors to be a complete, insightful, and inspiring new telling of the story of Christmas.

In *The Star*, we discover *magupati*, or the magi, who first realized that something of historic significance was taking place. Real people who studied the stars and served wealthy masters and kings with their interpretations, who left comfortable livings a thousand miles away to follow a star.

And while they did, a humble village girl and her betrothed husband-to-be were having their simple lives changed forever, historically awaiting the birth of a God-child.

There is much consternation and misunderstanding over the virgin pregnancy of Mary. And traditions—laws—that could have had her put to death. Despite this, Mary makes a perilous journey with her husband Joseph, arriving in the most unlikely of places, and thus becoming an unexpected, central person in humanity's journey. All the while, Mary and Joseph become the objects of the wrath of a wicked despot.

As in any historical story, we can only surmise what it would have been like to *be there*. And so, to further understand and perhaps *feel* the story, we immerse ourselves in it. Did it happen as we believe it did? What would it all look like, sound like, and perhaps even *smell* like? Who would we meet?

History tells us much. Inspiration fills in the gaps.

The people of Bethlehem, where this was all to have taken place, were simple people—village people. It was their lives that were disrupted by Mary and Joseph's arrival, then forever changed because of them.

We can imagine the everyday townspeople, their leaders, their lives, their history, even matters of faith that governed them. We can try to say who they were, including the shepherds they hired to tend to the vast natural fields and flocks around their town. Through it, we can gain insight into life there—before and as these events happened.

This historic story has many villains, none more than the legendary King Herod the Great, a merciless, maniacal tyrant who ruled over the nation of Israel at the bidding of Rome. At the time of our story, many soldiers—Roman occupiers as well as temple brigades—patrolled the streets, interfering with the people's lives.

There was treachery at every corner. There was a world about to implode, not unlike our own today.

It is our prayer that in *The Star of Bethlehem* we have a fresh, new, and much needed re-telling of the Christmas story.

It is hoped that, in some way, every reader would be touched by this telling of the story, and perhaps even moved to tell others about it, as the people we will meet did, many millennia ago.

# Chapter One
## The Wanderer's Dance

---

*Sabra, in Chaldea, Persia*
*Evening, in a star-filled sky*

The desert skies hide little at night.

From his open portico in the palace, Melchior could clearly identify every celestial visitor to the night sky, as he had done for nearly fifty years.

Melchior had been following some particular movements for several months now. He had seen an unusual rising in the east making its way across the desert sky—a sudden, bright arrival that surprised him one evening during his observations. Over many weeks, he tracked the planet from its rising to its zenith in the eastern sky. It was Jupiter.

It started in silence, unnoticeable to most everyone. A journey begun in an entirely unassuming yet splendid way to those who observed.

From his vantage point on the upper corner of the palace, he had been able to track a rendezvous taking shape, a celestial coming together. Most unusual, even for this veteran stargazer—in complete obscurity despite its unusual brightness in the crisp eastern sky. Unobstructed, always observing, he made notes of their movements. Nightly charting their course, the path to their destination soon began to startle him.

"Astounding," he was heard to say. Remphin had heard many wondrous descriptions over the years—some portending trouble, some splendor. But this was different.

As a priestly caste, Melchior was well accustomed to following the heavenly movements of planets, stars, constellations, even comets. His counsel was sought by kings and rulers, all seeking insight into celestial signs that would affect everything from war and famine to the new eras of history.

Indeed, he was not alone in these observations.

Caravans from the west in Arabia and further east in India had carried messages from sages and other *magupati* regarding observations of these new and unprecedented movements in the heavens. To the *magupati*, these movements, invisible to the general populace, were messages from the heavens. What was revealed by heaven had profound implications here on earth.

Jupiter was heading westward.

In its dance across the heavens, the planet was seen to stop and then reverse direction! In a period of almost nine months, the *magupati* observed Jupiter appearing to circle over Regulus, then appearing, as they observed, to create a crown, or "halo," over this "king star." As Jupiter continued its journey across the skies, it conjoined with Regulus, the "king's star," not once, but three times!

But to their astonishment, this heavenly dance did not end there.

In its third journey, Jupiter aligned with Venus, the mother star, until on one summer evening the two stars drew closer and closer, joining in a celestial "kiss," fusing into one brilliant star in the western sky. The sun was in Virgo.

Never before or since had these observations been recorded. To Melchior, heaven itself was speaking. And the implications were, in his sight, nothing short of epic, historic.

But what *was* heaven saying? To be sure, it would appear that a king was about to appear. But who? Where?

Kings ascend and kingdoms change. But to Melchior and those who had been observing these stars, the heavens had never announced such an arrival in such glorious, unmistakable fashion. Across time and space, Jupiter and Venus conjoining. To the learned seer, heaven itself was announcing a birth; not just for Persia, or India, but perhaps something more universal. A king of all kings, a king of all nations, a universal leader? Or something more—a warrior king, or the Son of the most high God?

They were astounded beyond excitement. Never in their lives had such an occurrence been observed. In all their careers, nothing like this. Still, to be validated, they needed to decipher the fullest meaning of what they had been observing. Not since the time of Zartosht several centuries before had any such recording been made that was even close. There was simply no precedent or occurrence to draw from to explain what was plainly evident—to them—in the east, in the evening sky.

Melchior began to write down his observations and insights and hastily dispatched his wards. One to Caspar in the east, in India, one to Hormisdas of Assyria, Basanater of Ethiopia, and Balthassar of Alexandria. Were they observing, as he was, this developing conjunction in the skies?

Did they too see this as an announcement of this king of kings, or were they deciphering this to simply be the announcement of an event that would in some way herald something new, or change *something* among the nations?

Over time, Melchior recorded every detail of the events unfolding in the heavens. Often, he was astounded at the paths, turns, and twists this heavenly wanderer would take. Through it, he discerned even more from these stars, and their co-stars, in this unfolding drama. Over the next several weeks, he began to anticipate their movements.

At times he could not eat, for reasons he did not understand. He took no visitors. His excitement was uncontainable, his focus singular for many days.

Daily, he waited for night and slept during the day. His preoccupation grew, as if this celestial happening was speaking to him alone.

Prophesy, or interpretation, is confirmed by the coming of events foreseen. More often, in the astrological sciences, it is confirmed by the witness of others, those whose observations concur with those of the seer. If indeed Balthassar and others were observing these events, what would *their* interpretation be?

Melchior was troubled. He was living in the time of such events that would serve as validation of the expertise with which he plied his lifetime craft. He was afforded great wealth and influence by his patrons for the observations he made, and the learned, reliable interpretations he made on their behalf.

Often, his patrons made bold decisions—at great cost—based on the counsel of Melchior. Yet with these "stars," an uncertain, almost confusing sense overwhelmed him. How would he relay this to them? How would this affect them here in Persia? Was this king to be for all people? Would this king take thrones and principalities—here in Persia, perhaps to the great consternation or disadvantage of his benefactors or to the king?

And how would *his* world change with this heralding event? He was caught between profound observation and consequence, and the uncertainty of personal effect.

Several centuries before, in nearby Babylon, King Cyrus had been hailed as the leader of leaders, the omnipotent. Indeed, even in Melchior's time, the great ruler and self-proclaimed son of the divine, Augustus of Rome, had declared a peace throughout the Roman world to celebrate his omnipotence and a peace (for some) throughout his empire.

But neither had planets dancing in anticipation of their coming.

He recalled that in Cyrus' time, Cyrus had shown mercy to a people he had conquered in the west, descendants of a Chaldean who professed homage to a single God; a God who had brought this people centuries later out of bondage in Egypt and given them lands in Canaan and the surrounding deserts, displacing many nations much stronger than they.

He was drawn to this.

It had been written in other ancient texts that the Chaldeans were known to be sorcerers, so their connection to an everlasting *single* God he could not understand; he feared this god could be a sorcerer, or the evil one himself. Cyrus had plundered their kingdom decades before, yet for some unknown reason had allowed these people to return to their homes years after possessing them, even helping them rebuild their walled cities.

Remphin remembered hearing that this people had in their writings a tradition that their God, in the fullness of time, was to provide them a deliverer, a savior—a "Messiah." Melchior possessed a scroll which he had Remphin search for. It was believed to contain the writings of one of their prophets. It had been translated for him by a Greek priest several decades before, when Melchior was just a young man beginning to divine the stars.

Remphin returned with the very scroll. Upon opening the scroll, he observed something which startled him:

> *"For unto us a Child is born, unto us a Son is given; And the government will be upon His shoulder. And His name will be called Wonderful, Counselor, Mighty God, Everlasting Father, Prince of Peace. Of the increase of His government and peace, there will be no end."*[1]
>
> *- Isaias*

In Melchior's own tradition, his Saoshyans pointed to a leader who would miraculously be born of a virgin in a time of chaos. In the fullness of time, this king would defeat evil itself. Melchior had long forgotten this. Upon reading further, he could not believe his eyes:

> *"Behold, the virgin shall be with child and bear a Son, and they shall call His name Immanuel, which is translated, 'God with us.'"*[2]

God—*with us?*

In his own beloved Persia, it was recorded that He who was revered as the one true God had rescued a nation to the west. This nation called itself the true holy people, the sons of God Himself, the Ancient of days. Indeed, in the writings of a certain woman of their people, a queen of sorts, centuries before, he himself had read this. Though he did not possess full knowledge of this people's history, Melchior was fascinated by these writings and kept them in his library.

Melchior—as well as other Persians—were familiar with the Canaanites' quest; unprecedented victories against much stronger enemies, where it was said this God fought *for* them. Yet it seemed these people had a history of rebelling against this "one true God," often hastening their own captivities from among the great nations of the region. He could not understand the paradox.

Melchior reckoned then that perhaps these heavenly harbingers were for some other country, perhaps farther to the west, perhaps a resurrection of the empire of Egypt? Midian, or one across the great Arabian wilderness far from his homeland? Or could it be lands across the great sea?

He considered that perhaps the easiest explanation would be the fulfillment of Augustus' Roman vision of peace. Perhaps the heavens were confirming this too.

Melchior considered and studied. Jupiter about to enter Virgo would mean a king about to be born—to a goddess, or in the womb of a woman?

Augustus was already a grown man. No king's birth—not pharaoh's, or Cyrus', Nimrod's, Nebuchadnezzar's—not Sheba of Ethiopia, the great Solomon, Alexander of Macedon, or even Caesar himself had had their birth heralded by celestial events.

"Remphin, were not sons of Judah brought into the courts of Nebuchadnezzar to interpret his dreams, in his time?" Melchior queried his assistant. "Didn't he make them to serve him as Chaldeans, though they were loyal to this one God?"

Remphin dispatched without further direction from Melchior and came to the repository of writings in the palace where they lived.

Sometime later, he returned with the scrolls of Belteshazzar, one of the youths Nebuchadnezzar had carried off from Jehoiakim, King of Judah, after he had laid siege to Jerusalem.

"This youth was found to have extraordinary gifts for interpretation," Remphin said as he read. "But it appears he and his cohorts were punished by the king several times for continuing to follow that God of Judah."

"These rebels, as was thought in his court, were thrown into a den of lions, yet emerged unharmed. And again, thrown into a furnace so hot it killed the men who threw them into it. Yet again, they emerged unharmed. Who could have done this except this one true God himself, or His angel who was with them?"

Melchior stood pondering the words Remphin explained.

As the two men stood, they were interrupted by the sudden opening of the door. "The caravans from Ghandaria, Melchior; they've arrived."

Melchior made his way with haste down to the courtyard of the palace. He offered his greeting to the merchants and the stewards of their house. "A wonderful journey, lord," offered one of the stewards. "Fruitful, with a full account," the steward said, handing Melchior a written account of the goods the caravan had delivered.

As they began to unload their caravans, a stately, familiar figure emerged from behind the caravan. "I wondered if you would come, old friend," smiled Melchior, as he made his way with increasing haste to greet the visitor. He smiled and breathed deeply as he embraced the man, equally as far along in age as himself. "Come, Caspar; you must be tired."

Caspar was an unusually tall and regal man. Though having made the arduous journey from the east, he was impeccably dressed in resplendent finery, looking just as ready to meet a head of state as to join his friend for supper. It was no coincidence that he was here.

As they entered the upper room, Caspar closed the door behind them. Without so much as a word of discussion prior to entering the room, Caspar stopped, turned around, and looked Melchior directly in the eye. "It is the king of the Israelites of Canaan, Melchior. I am certain."

Both men stood silent. Without a further word among them, both men made their way to Melchior's private dining room. "Come, my friend, you must be hungry." Melchior gestured to his friend to recline.

"I am hungry, Melchior, but for more than food," the man returned. "Who are we, that in our lifetimes such a thing could happen? Yet the world sleeps—unnoticing, unaware."

Both men bowed their heads, almost in quiet confirmation. They were elated to share these observations and the realized wonderment of the events happening above them.

"Caspar, just this day I found the writings of a Judean, writing in captivity barely five hundred years ago," Melchior said. "Remphin brought me the scroll. He saw this: this man prophesied that the Messiah would come in 483 years. Is he exact in his calculations? Are the stars foretelling this to us, in our time? But I do not understand how this would be possible, that the eternal God of heaven would do this to this smallest of nations; that this one God whom these people wrestle with still thinks of them, to deliver them this Messiah. Their God is truly worthy of their trust, their faith."

"But there it is, Melchior. I am confident others will make a journey too, to find this king," Caspar said. "I have read in their writings from their great prophet:

*"From Midian, Epha and Sheba they will come, bringing their gifts of gold and incense to proclaim the praises of the Lord, to glorify the house of His glory!"*[3]

"And in another place, in the writings of Musa their greatest prophet who led them out of centuries of bondage to Pharaoh, I found this:

*"I see Him, but not now. I behold him, but not near. A star shall come out of Jacob, a scepter shall rise out of Israel."*[4]

"What—or who—will we find there, Caspar?" Melchior asked. "A child? A man? Power? It will not be easy for a man; their king is ruthless, and Roman rule in that region is oppressive. Caesar casts a keen eye on these outskirts of his empire and tolerates no rebellion. But if this is of God…" Melchior hesitated before continuing.

As a Persian astrologer, could he travel westward to where the star would lead him and his friend? Would they be welcomed there, or dismissed?

They anticipated that a conjunction of Jupiter and Venus in a morning sky would see this "star" rise in the eastern sky, but because of their orbits, they would come together as one star in the northwest some months later.

"These are the wanderers of heaven, Melchior," Caspar said. "But it is we who are the wanderers."

---

The journey westward would take Melchior, Caspar, and their entourages many weeks, if not months, to travel the nearly one thousand miles west.

"We will prepare for the journey, Caspar. We will leave with haste in three days' time."

His guest replied: "May the God of heaven Himself— and His star—be our guide."

# Chapter Two
# House of Bread

The quaint little town sat quietly against the eastern hill-side, on the outskirts of the Judean wilderness.

Since the times of their judges many centuries before, the village had stood amidst vast natural fields of grain which the people harvested each year for their subsistence and trade. Bethlehem had been known for centuries as the source of much of the nation's grain, its bread, from the vast wheat and barley fields its citizens plied.

This "house," founded by the patriarchal Kind David many centuries earlier, was small among the nation's towns and villages. Yet throughout its history, Bethlehem stood quietly, front and center to the battles, dramas, and recordings of the nation's comings and goings. It was said that this town would one day produce an extraordinary king, in David's line, one that it was said: *"Would one day rule the nation and peoples forever."*

In this present time, the people were preparing for the celebration of the Feast of Channukah, a festival "of light" which had been celebrated for a hundred years or so, a celebration "of light" to commemorate a victory over another invading king and a miracle that took place for the people.

Concurrently with Augustus Caesar's census taking place this year, revelrous soldiers and Roman officials who were overseeing the registrations were simultaneously celebrating an ancient, very Roman festival of Saturnalia. It was the most anticipated week of the Roman calendar, celebrated each year during the winter solstice. Ironically, Saturnalia celebrated the return of light as well, as the solstice hastened days of longer light's return.

This year's Saturnalia had additional meaning to Romans. Augustus, seeing himself as the "Father of the Country," indeed of the entire world, had declared himself "Pater Patria," giving honor to himself as what he referred to as the "Prince of Peace." There was little unrest throughout the empire, and Augustus made sure the people saw him as responsible for it. The revelry throughout Bethlehem, in Jerusalem, and indeed through-out the world, celebrating Saturnalia and Augustus, was widespread and decadent.

---

Back in the center of the town, Zechariah and his family were making preparations for the feast. Zechariah was the rabbi of the small synagogue in Bethlehem which had stood in the town since ancient times. Tradition in the little town held that where the synagogue stood this day was the original site of the first synagogue there, in the days of the ancestors.

Though ravaged and destroyed in many conquests by the Assyrians, the Persians, the Babylonians, and others, this stubborn people always rebuilt their house of worship to their God. The small building was the center of their community, an unwavering dedication to the God of Israel throughout every age and time.

It was said that King David himself had directed the priestly Levite class to establish this house of worship in the town that King David would call his home base. The Ark of the Covenant, the feared vessel of power and preservation built in the time of Moses and Aaron, was said to have been brought there as well, many centuries before.

Bethlehem, though indeed a small, seemingly unimportant village to the Romans and others, meant much to the Jews. It was in this small village that the sons of Israel, who longed for their Redeemer, memorialized the words of an ancient sufferer crying out to his God:

*"If only there were a mediator between us, someone who could bring us together. If there is a messenger for him, a mediator, one among a thousand, to show man His uprightness, then He is gracious to him, and says, 'Deliver him from going down to the Pit; I have found a ransom.'"*[5]

The people lived by faith. They were the children of the most high God, His chosen. It was their culture to believe that the words of the ancients would one day become true in their midst.

———

Zechariah's house was adjacent to the synagogue. A meager, simple home, but Zechariah's wife Esther made it a welcoming home for their family and the many residents and visitors to Bethlehem. Esther could be found, often, kneading barley or wheat into loaves. She supplied the bread to her family as well as for the many feasts and needs of this small community.

On this particular day, Esther was at the oven when a loud rattle and bang broke the stillness of the home. Esther looked to the corner of the room near the window.

"You rascal," she said, startled. "You scared me half to death!"

Picking himself up from the floor, a young child of about ten brushed himself off and stood up slowly. "I'm sorry, Esther. I thought the table was under the window," the young boy exclaimed, somewhat embarrassed at his fall and the clamor he had caused.

A mere moment later, the door of the house swung open slowly, revealing an even younger boy. He stood for a moment in the doorway. "Peath be on this houth," the little boy extolled, with a wistful little lisp. Esther smiled.

"And… 'peath'… be to you, David," she smiled. "You can come in," Esther said, welcoming the child.

Little David was a frail boy of about seven. His legs were twisted, and he stood with the help of two makeshift crutches, the tops wrapped in tattered, well-worn cloths, one under each armpit. As he leaned forward to enter, David's entry was interrupted by Jonathan. "I promise not to come in through the window anymore, Esther." She simply smiled in return.

Jonathan and David were frequent visitors to Zechariah and Esther's house. They would often stop by when in the village. Esther always awaited their visits with a motherly anticipation. She loved to see them, despite Jonathan's frequently disruptive entries. He loved her as well, and regularly played a game of trying to catch her off guard to announce his arrival.

They loved listening to Zechariah's frequent stories of hope, of deliverance, of the promise of an end to oppression and want. This struck a chord with these little boys. Zechariah and Esther's family were grown and had families of their own. The young boys brought joy to Esther and a welcome respite from the duties of synagogue and worship.

The boys also knew there would always be food there.

With the festival approaching, they were determined to visit with these two elderly patrons of theirs, and to get some freshly baked bread to take back to the fields where the boys spent most of their time. As this first day of the eight-day feast approached, on this occasion there would also be *latkes*—special potato pancakes, and *sufganiyot*—delicious fried donuts the boys loved. Esther generously dished out some of the recently cooked treats to the boys, who proceeded to devour them with haste. "Go slowly," she implored. "You're going to get more on your face than in your mouths!" she exclaimed, wiping some oil and sugar from David's already messy face.

As the sweet feast continued, the door opened once again. Zechariah arrived in the house, accompanied by two children and a teenage girl, the boy and girl's guardian, or sitter, of sorts. "Someone's up to no good, I believe," he directed to the boys before glancing over to Esther with a wistful glance.

"Rabbi, we have visitors," she replied with a proud smile.

"I see," he replied, looking at the boys. "You remember Aman and Atalia, don't you, Jonathan and David?"—who barely looked up, continuing to devour the donuts with relish.

Zechariah smiled and raised his eyebrows. "Come, children; let's get you some treats before they're all gone!"

As the children and Sarah, their sitter, ate, Esther continued her preparations. Zechariah went about his own work.

From behind a worn and dusty tapestry he brought out a stand of sorts, taking it out from the cloth in which it was stored. As he began to set up the stand, he began to place eight oil lamps on it, one on each branch of the stand.

"Aman, Atalia, do you know what these are?" Zechariah asked.

Aman and Atalia were the children of Elimelech, one of the town's wealthiest and most affluent citizens. They spent a lot of time at study. Aman looked up respectfully and said, "The festival lights, Rabbi."

Zechariah turned to Atalia and asked, "And do you know why we light the lights each year, Atalia?" Jonathan jumped in, as if an eager child in class: "Because the oil didn't run out," the boy exclaimed. Zechariah, pausing for a moment, acknowledged the interrupting boy's answer.

"Gather round, children," Zechariah—ever the teacher—said, inviting them. The children and young Sarah all moved to the center of the room. Jonathan stuffed one last *sufganiyot* into his mouth, much to Esther's delight.

Zechariah reverently began to recount the story of Chanukkah to the children:

"Nearly two hundred years ago, our homeland was invaded by a king whose name was Antiochus Epiphanes. Can you say that, David?" The boy replied proudly, "On… tith…icus… Am…pifaneath!"

"Very good," Esther replied, smiling lovingly at her little friend.

Zechariah continued: "He came to try to convert our people to a different faith than that of our fathers. But the people wouldn't have it," he said. "One of our leaders, named Judas Maccabeus, fought against this king. For over three years, the fight went on."

The children all sat attentive, loving Zechariah's learned delivery.

"During the war, this king entered our temple and made it unholy. He tried to destroy it, but it would not be so. Judas and our patriots eventually defeated Antiochus and his army and drove them out of Judah."

On hearing this, little David clapped, applauding the victory. The rest smiled. "That is right, David, it was a happy time. God had once again delivered our people, as He has always promised He would."

"Judas did not like that the temple was desecrated," Esther contributed.

Zechariah continued: "So, when he drove them out, Judas entered the temple and found that there was only one small jar of oil left there that was not defiled by Antiochus. The jar had only enough oil left in it to burn for one day. This was important to our temple practices, and no one knew what to do.

"But then, a miracle happened."

The children's eyes opened a bit in eager anticipation of what the miracle could have been.

"When they lit the oil lamp with the olive oil, the oil burned for eight days!" Esther continued.

"Judas was able to find new sacred oil after that, so the temple could remain lit." Zechariah added: "Judas assembled the men of the land and cleaned the temple out. And they rebuilt the altar of the temple so that our worship for God could continue."

The children smiled and sighed a collective breath of confidence.

"Do you know why we celebrate this?" Zechariah asked the children.

He continued, "Because of the invasion, we couldn't celebrate Sukkoth, so we began to celebrate a new feast. We called it Chanukkah—the festival of lights."

David smiled, acknowledging his understanding of the meaning of the feast's name.

Zechariah finished: "Once Judas and the people cleansed the temple and rebuilt it, they dedicated it again to God. The day was 25 Kislev, in a couple of days! Judas then made a proclamation that this dedication should be celebrated every year around this time. Eight days of celebration for the eight days the oil kept the lamps lit."

"I want you to remember one more thing," their teacher added. "*Chanukkah*, in our language, means 'education.'" Esther smiled, knowing this was coming.

Zechariah, ever the teacher, continued: "Never forget that we celebrate our strength and our perseverance as a people. The light never runs out, and neither does our relationship to God, who watches over us—His people—always."

The children sat there for a moment, content.

"But why do you light the candles inside the house, Rabbi?" Jonathan asked innocently. "I see them outside at other people's houses."

"Some people don't like the fire," Zechariah replied. "And the wind blows them out and knocks them over sometimes. We don't want to make them feel bad." He smiled, acknowledging the question.

"Do we get presents now?" Jonathan added, changing the subject in an instant, and with a curious smile, knowing the answer.

"Yes," Esther interjected maternally. She loved to give the children gifts during the season, especially to the boys. "Today we give sweets and a shekel each. Remember to share your gift with those who are without, as well," she instructed, knowing the boys had nothing and the other children plenty.

Zechariah brought out a *sevivon* for the children to play with.

The Chanukkah *sevivon* had inscribed on it these words: *nes gadol haya sham*, which means: "a great miracle happened there," a constant reminder to the children playing with it of the eight days the lamps stayed lit. But it was the cakes the boys relished the most.

---

Undoubtedly, Beth-le'hem of Ephrathah became "the House of Bread" in recognition of this natural abundance of barley and wheat, celebrated especially this time of year. In years to come, "the House of Bread" would take on even greater meaning.

As Zechariah turned to leave the house to attend to his duties, Jonathan, as could be predicted, stuffed his pockets with some of the *latkes* and *sufganiyot* Esther had quietly wrapped in a cloth and handed to him. He rushed out the door as if in a whirlwind, nearly knocking Zechariah over.

He paused only a few steps outside to wait for his younger brother to catch up to him. The elder brother then ran ahead down the dusty road toward the edge of town, while his brother hobbled as quickly as he could on his two crutches to keep up with him.

Esther stood at the doorway, watching the young boys as they made their way down the dusty road. Her mind wandered as she thought so lovingly about them. But her heart ached for David. A slight smile came across her face as she watched the little guy hobble away as quickly as anyone could on those crutches. In the silence of her heart, she again asked God to help him.

# Chapter Three
## Magnificat

---

The Galilean groves glisten green in the time of harvest. Many people can be seen coming to and from the hillsides and fields just outside of town. In the distant horizon, the tall buildings of Sepphoris can be seen, the metropolitan center of commerce in this rustic outpost.

The heat of the day slows the pace of life here. A young woman can be seen sitting outside her home, crushing grain in a crude stone mortar. As she does, her husband and his young apprentice are working on a home, one that had been begun several years earlier, building an upper room on an almost completed stone structure in the middle of town. They are of modest means in this small hillside town: she, a woman in her late teens; he, a bit older.

As they work, a regal carriage of sorts can be seen making its way up the stone-lined dirt road that leads up the hill. In it, an elder of the ruling religious class from Jerusalem is being accompanied by a young physician. There is a sense of anticipation, their journey hastened by unusual events that had happened several years earlier, one hundred miles away in Judea.

As the carriage stops, the driver gets out to assist the middle-aged man. The physician follows and as he exits, turns to survey the area nearby. He is a tall, charismatic man in his own right, dressed modestly, but clean. His appearance is that of some accomplishment or profession.

The elder has been anticipating this visit for some time. In fact, it has been a journey of sorts for him for quite a few years. The younger physician has in mind to investigate the events further, perhaps to record an orderly account.

Gamaliel is of a sect called the pharisees. Together with the high priests and elders in the temple at Jerusalem, theirs is the task of keeping the faith of the people in practice. This, despite the country's occupation by the Romans. There's is an uneasy—some would say *unholy*—alliance with the Roman governors and the puppet king they have installed to rule for them.

For both the elder and younger man, as they approach the woman, there is a bit of reverence steeped in their tradition. It is a time when men rarely speak with women, by law and tradition, especially for religious leaders.

"Are you Mary?" the physician asks. "Yes," the woman replies. She is neither afraid nor intimidated by the introduction, but simply and modestly looks up at the man addressing her. She has been expecting them.

"I am Luke," the young man directs toward her with his introduction. "I was pleased to hear you would be willing to see me."

For the moment, the pharisee stays a few steps behind at the carriage, looking hesitantly at the two who are meeting for the first time.

Mary gets up and brushes the dust off her garment, a modest piece tied with a sash around the waist. She lifts the outer piece over her shoulders and brings it to rest on her head. "May I get you some water?" she asks. "You must be thirsty from your journey." Luke responds with a simple smile in the affirmative. She glances toward Gamaliel, who hesitates a second or two, nods, and gives a similar affirmation. He then moves slowly toward them.

"I am Joseph," her husband says, turning from his work, putting down his tools for a moment, and brushing off the stone and wood dust on him. He bows his head slightly toward the two men. Mary returns with a pitcher of cool water and some cups for the guests and her husband. They sit at a small wooden table and chairs in the courtyard outside the house in a small, rustic garden of colorful flowers and herbs.

"Please," Joseph says, motioning them toward the chairs. "They haven't gotten much use since I finished them." He smiles. Gamaliel continues to appear just slightly uncomfortable, being so intimately in conversation with ordinary people. Nonetheless, he slowly sits down as well and nods in appreciation to Mary for the water.

"Mary, there is much word about in the city and the countryside regarding, shall I say, your visit to Bethlehem during the census some years ago," Luke begins. "I must admit, if what is spoken about is even partially true, I am humbly intrigued. The implications are great for the nation—indeed, beyond these borders."

Mary picks her head up a bit, slowly, and replies with a nod of her head.

"May I ask you... what... how..." Luke begins, not sure how to approach the questioning.

"How did this come about?" Mary replies assuredly, finishing his thought for him.

"Yes," he says, breathing a sigh of relief. "Thank you. I don't know where to begin."

———

Mary begins:

"I have a cousin, Elizabeth, who lives some distance from here. She is much older than I. She and her husband, Zacharias, did not have any children. It was believed at that time that Elizabeth could not conceive. I'm not certain. I believe they both had given up on having children many years earlier, though they stayed devoted to each other and to his work in the temple. Privately they still prayed that she would have a child, even in her old age."

"I know this man," Gamaliel injects, hearing about temple work. "He has been about temple service for quite some time. A good man," he adds.

Mary smiles and glances toward the elder, their eyes making contact for the first time since the arrival of the two men.

"I'm sorry," the elder offers. "I shouldn't have interrupted you." Still looking in his direction, Mary simply and respectably smiles again. There is great anticipation between the men and Mary that causes a bit of awkwardness early in the conversation.

"Elizabeth told some of us later that Zacharias had entered the temple one day in his time of service," Mary continues. "He entered the Holy of Holies, as was the custom, and offered the incense and prayers for the people, many of which had, of course, gathered outside the temple to pray.

"Zacharias did not like to talk about it, even later. But it is said that he was startled by a sudden white light that illuminated the chamber. This was unusual. He turned and saw the angel of the Lord standing there, on the right side of the altar. Zacharias was initially overcome with fear and fell to his knees. He could not believe his eyes. He was trembling."

"Did he ever describe the angel?" Luke asks.

"Yes," Mary responds. "He did, to Elizabeth. A beautiful man, imbued with the most beautiful light—the power and majesty of God, she recounted. He was larger than a man, though as a man in appearance. The angel realized that Zacharias was very afraid and told him not to be afraid. After a moment or so, this seemed to calm Zacharias."

"What did the angel say?" Gamaliel asks, in nervous awe of the story being told, as one who serves in the temple as well.

"'Your prayer has been heard,' he said. 'Your wife Elizabeth will bear you a son. You will call his name John. You will be filled with joy, and many will praise God for him, for he is going to be great in God's sight." Mary hesitantly looked around to the men. "He will be filled with the Holy Spirit of the Lord from the time he is conceived. He is going to turn many of the children of our nation to the Lord,'" Mary says with pride, looking and turning to each of the men with gentle eye contact..

Joseph speaks, interrupting but reinforcing what his wife is saying to the men: "The angel told him he would go before the Lord in the spirit and power of Elijah the prophet, to make ready a people prepared for the Lord."

At the mention of Elijah, the elder man stands, stunned. He slowly leans forward.

Joseph continues: "Zacharias was not a man given to joking or discussing the absurd things that people often talk about. For a moment, he did not—could not—believe what the angel was saying to him. He and Elizabeth were well beyond the time of having children."

"How long did this—visit—last?" Luke asks, now looking down and writing notes on a tablet he had brought. Mary tells him that this went on for quite a few minutes, as Elizabeth and the people were growing a bit impatient outside, waiting for him to come out from the temple. Some had believed that perhaps he had suffered some illness, or had fallen.

"The angel simply addressed his seeming unbelief with: 'I am Gabriel, who stands in the presence of God,'" Mary says slowly, confidently, proudly—almost as if recalling the announcement herself. "The angel told Zacharias he was sent specifically for these purposes, which he called 'glad tidings.'"

Joseph says: "The angel told him that because of his disbelief—he had laughed—he would not be able to speak until these things were fulfilled. The people saw immediately upon his leaving the temple that something had happened. He could not speak. Some weeks later, his temple duties were completed, and he went home. He did not speak for months."

The group simply sits there for a moment, taking this all in. Gamaliel and Luke are trying to comprehend the significance of "the Holy Spirit" coming upon him, and what the "spirit and power of Elijah" could mean. Most of all, that Zacharias was told this by the angel Gabriel himself. They wonder what eventually happened, if the child was indeed born to this old woman, and how this relates to the story they have come to ascertain.

"How did you, Mary, and your family hear about this?" Luke asks.

At this question, Joseph slowly rises from the table and places his hand on Mary's shoulder. "You must excuse me," he says to the guests. "I must be about this house, here." With this, he smiles and looks down at Mary, then walks the several steps to rejoin his apprentice.

Mary glances at her husband as he walks away. She turns to the men and continues:

"It was about the time of the spring harvest. Many of us were in the fields gathering dates, figs, and olives. It was a happy time. We would gather from early in the morning and then sit under the groves, eating some of the fruit, laughing with friends, and enjoying each other.

"I had been betrothed to Joseph for only a few months, but was still living in my parents' home, the home of my youth. We had not as yet begun any preparations for the marriage, but Joachim, my father, had given permission for Joseph and me to wed."

---

She paused a few seconds, looking off, then continued: "I could not understand the wind one day. It was completely still. My friends had gone from the fields into town to bring what they had picked, and I had stayed behind, resting under the shade of a large olive tree I loved to sit under. As I sat there, my soul was at peace, prayerful; I sat looking out at the hills, thankful for the harvest and the rest. A wind came suddenly, unexpectedly, and blew my clothing. It woke me, of sorts, from my meditation. It was midday.

"As I sat there, looking up at the clouds to see if a storm was coming, I was startled by a man; not a normal man, but someone I had never seen before in Nazareth. I wasn't sure who he was. I wasn't really afraid, but I sat up from resting against the tree. He seemed to move toward me, though I did not really see him walk."

The two men are riveted to her recollections. She is so clear, so forthright, they have both believed her from early on.

She continues: "He told me: 'Rejoice,' that the Lord was with me, and that I was 'highly favored of God.'"

The two men look at each other, and each lowers his head for a brief moment before continuing to listen to the young woman.

"I could not understand what this meant," Mary says, as honest as a child. "He never really said his name, but I realized in my spirit that he was an angel of the Lord. I sat there, a bit amazed, I must admit. He seemed to know what I was thinking and reassured me with a gentleness of appearance and speech.

"'Behold,' he said, 'God has bestowed His blessing on you. You are going to conceive in your womb and bear a son. You are to call him Jesus,' he said. 'He will be great and will be called the Son of the Most High.' I thought, *God?*

"I was astonished by his speech and asked him how this was going to happen, as Joseph and I were observing our laws and had not been together, though we were espoused to each other.

"The angel did not hesitate, but simply responded that the Holy Spirit was going to come upon me, and that the power of God would overshadow me, so that this 'Holy One,' he called him, whom I would bear, would be called the Son of God."

At these words, the two men sit there, astounded, speechless. They look at each other. In some schools of thought, it was blasphemy for a mere person to put themselves on the level of God. They look to each other again. Neither one of them can speak. It is not disbelief, or an intention to indict her.

The men are understandably in awe. Her sincerity was apparent, they would both later recall. They would both acknowledge feeling a sense of some astonishment, mixed with a private hope that this could even possibly be true.

After a minute or two, Gamaliel asks her to continue. Mary continues: "It was the angel who told me about Elizabeth. He said that she had also conceived a son, even in her old age, and was already in her sixth month. She had kept this quiet for five months for fear of ridicule by the people. He told me that this had happened to her; he called her 'one who was called barren,' to show her—and assure me—that nothing with God would be impossible.

"I believed him and was overcome by the Spirit, which uttered from within me without thought:

*"Behold the maidservant of the Lord! Let it be to me according to your word."*⁶

"The angel smiled and bowed his head at my acknowledgement. I can't remember at any time thereafter if he spoke audibly. It was as if his message, his words, penetrated my soul and my mind. In an instant, I was aware of the wonder of this, but still humbled and uncertain as to why God had chosen me."

"Had you engaged in any great study of the sacred scriptures before, Mary?" Gamaliel asks. Perhaps he is looking to see if she is recalling words she was familiar with before the encounter.

She gently purses her lips and nods her head: "Some," she replies. "As much as any girl my age."

"Are you aware of the writings of Isaias?" he asks cautiously.

"I didn't consider them at the time, until after the angel had left. *'Who would believe our report...?'*" she asks, as if it is a question she has pondered, directing this short scripture quote to her elder unpretentiously. Gamaliel looks her right in the eye and continues, slowly, from Isaias' words:

> *"Surely, He has borne our sicknesses and carried our pains; He was wounded for our transgressions."*[7]

*"By His stripes, we are healed?"* she says proudly, continuing from Isaias as if asking Gamaliel a question. She concludes, with a slight smile: *"He shall see the labor of His soul and be satisfied."*

The three pause a moment. Mary seems to reflect on this. "Surely, I have pondered what this, my Child, has come to do." The three sit in stark silence.

She continues, determinedly, her recollections of the encounter with the angel: "My spirit was alive within me while the angel was still there. I felt deeply these words, as if they were about someone else:

> *"My soul declares the greatness of the Lord, and my spirit rejoices in God my Savior. The Lord has regarded the lowly estate of his maidservant; for behold, henceforth all generations will call me blessed."*[8]

She continues without hesitation, recalling her spirit speaking that day:

*"He who is mighty has done great things for me. And holy is His name. His mercy is on those who fear Him, from generation to generation. He has scattered the proud in the imaginations of their hearts and exalted the lowly. He has remembered His mercy to our fathers, to Abraham and to his seed forever."*

"I remember these words to this day," she says to her visitors. "I fell forward, exhausted from the encounter. When I looked up, the angel had gone away, and I was alone. I sat there, wonderfully at peace, yet…" For a moment, Mary was far away in her thoughts, then said, "I would see him again."

She sees the look of wonder on the men.

"I have so many questions," Gamaliel acknowledges, in childlike fashion, far more innocently and somewhat beneath his position. He no longer seems to care. Mary simply smiles heartily. Luke nods and smiles himself, speechless at what is being given to them, recording her words all the while.

"Shall we walk?" Mary suggests.

The trio gets up from the table and begins to walk the short, dusty road out of town, into the fields where, a few short years before, Mary had been visited by the angel.

"I've never been to Nazareth," Gamaliel notes as they enter the fields, trying to make small talk.

"It is home," she replies, walking comfortably, barefoot, between the two men.

"Joseph is of the house of David, is he not?" Gamaliel says.

"Yes," Mary responds.

"Is this why you and he travelled to Bethlehem for the census?" he continues.

"Yes, but not immediately," she adds.

"I didn't know who to talk to, or even if I should talk about the angel. My mother must have known something, but she did not ask. Joseph too. He was so busy trying to build the house and take care of his customers from Sepphoris that he often worked well into the night. I could not add that to his burden. I wanted to tell my friends, but I didn't, perhaps thinking they wouldn't believe me either."

Luke asks: "You must have felt very alone, Mary?"

"Not really," Mary replies, her eyes and slight, honest smile mirroring her inner thoughts, her belief that she was never really alone.

"I did feel an overwhelming sense that I had to see Elizabeth," Mary continues. "She would be late in her time and perhaps would need some help. I felt inside myself that I was supposed to be in attendance at her son's birth as well. I felt... that our children were going to be tied together in some way, in this greater purpose somehow, in a way I did not fully understand."

"Did your parents accompany you?" Luke asks.

"No, I made the journey alone," she adds. "Well, not totally alone. A couple from our village were making the trip into the hill country, and I was able to join them. I assured my family I would return shortly."

"How long did you stay?" Luke asks.

"It turned out that I stayed there about three months," Mary responds.

"May I tell you something—something I haven't told anyone?" she asks, almost playfully, of both men.

"Please…!" they respond, each with a little bit of a laugh—as if everything to this point was not enough!

"Their home in Judea is in a very modest little town, not too far from Jerusalem," she continues. "I had only been there once before. I was admiring the hillsides on the road leading to the town when we came to the outskirts where Elizabeth and Zacharias live. I remembered their house from my visit years before. I stepped down off the wagon we were travelling on. I thanked my travelling companions and walked toward the front door.

"As I opened the door, I saw Elizabeth first. We both smiled at her unusual condition. I offered my cousin greetings and went to embrace her. She suddenly stepped back and held her stomach, with an awkward look on her face.

"'Oooooo…' she said. Her baby jumped inside her, almost as if hearing my voice. It was funny, at first. But

Elizabeth began to speak loudly, unusually, in the Spirit. I am not comfortable saying this, but she exclaimed:

*"Hail to you, my sister. And blessed are you among women, Mary; blessed is the fruit of your womb! But why has this been granted to me that the mother of my Lord should come to me?"*[10]

"Elizabeth did not know that I was with child, so her greeting startled me, but just for a second.

"'I wanted to be here, Elizabeth,' I replied.

"Elizabeth continued to speak in the Spirit:

*"For indeed, as soon as the voice of your greeting sounded in my ears, the babe leaped in my womb for joy. Blessed are you for believing the Lord that those things you have been told will be fulfilled."*[11]

"We embraced, and Elizabeth took my hands and brought them toward her stomach. The child in her moved toward me, or should I say toward the baby within me, bulging her already extended stomach farther. It was a moment I will never forget."

"Where was Zacharias during this time?" Gamaliel asks. "Did you see him?"

"Zacharias was not speaking still, almost the whole time I was there," Mary replies. "He used a small tablet to write things to me he wanted to say. I enjoyed spending time with them, helping in their fields, around their house. They had many friends who seemed to be genuinely excited for her to deliver."

"Did her delivery progress normally?" Luke adds. "I mean, did she have any complications, given her age?"

"When her day came, she seemed to know it was time," Mary continues. "She helped some of the women and me prepare the space for her to deliver. Her pains were regular and growing in frequency. She handled her delivery very well.

"When it came time for her child to be born, Elizabeth simply cried out in a loud voice and gave birth quickly to her son. The child cried very loudly upon coming out, so much so that it startled all of us in the room, not the least of which was Elizabeth. We all laughed together. 'God's voice, for sure!' Elizabeth exclaimed, though none of the other women were aware of what she meant, assuming she was making an off-handed comment about her child and her age."

"And Zacharias?" Gamaliel asks.

"Zacharias and the men outside with him heard the child's wail and began to clap their hands. The women inside ululated loudly, making the traditional birth chant together, to announce the child's birth.

"After giving the baby to Elizabeth, one of the neighbors in attendance asked Elizabeth what the child's name was to be. From her birth bed she said, 'His name will be John.' At that moment, Zacharias entered between the curtains to see his son. There was no small matter among the people in the room over the name.

"I had wished that the people would give her some time before bringing this up, but I assume, given the matter, that there was much anticipation among them. I felt badly, though, as this older woman had just given birth. They continued to raise the issue of the child's name. 'But you have no one in your family with this name,' they said. Elizabeth repeated: 'His name will be John.'

"They turned to Zacharias, still mute from the encounter with the angel in the temple. He wrote on a tablet: 'John.' Immediately, he was no longer mute and spoke for the first time in months: 'His name is John,' he spoke. All stood astonished at Zacharias' sudden speaking. All gave praise to God for His faithfulness and for giving Elizabeth and Zacharias a child in their old age."

"Did you stay? I mean, when did you decide to leave and return home to Nazareth?" Luke asks.

"After a few more weeks, I decided it was time to return to Nazareth and my family and Joseph. I began to be a bit anxious, not only about the journey, but about the fact that I was beginning to show. They still did not know; only Elizabeth and Zacharias knew. I, at times, was worried that they would not believe me as to this Child's origins. Yet I was comforted in the spirit by our

God, and knew that as He had made the way for Elizabeth, so would He make the way for me."

Upon hearing the totality of the story that happened in Judea, Gamaliel takes several steps and moves away from the tree they have stopped to sit under. Quietly, believing, he begins to consider the words of the sacred writings that would pertain to this Child. "This is astounding," he says aloud, to himself.

He turns back to the other two: "John was a miracle, for sure. Yours indeed is only a child too, Mary. Yet everything we hope for as a nation rests on Him. I don't mean to burden you, Mary, but essentially, you are telling us that this Child is the One—the One from of old—He who is destined for the rise and fall of many in Israel. I believe you. I do."

He is a bit perplexed, trying to reckon this, as he continues: "Have you considered how you can possibly train this Child? How will Joseph raise Him? How will he prepare for this? And when will this Child show Himself? As a child? A man? I'm sorry…"

Mary simply smiles at Gamaliel's anxious questions.

She seems to reassure them with words from the sacred writings to her visitors.

"Does this help, Rabbi?

*"Therefore, the Lord Himself will give you a sign: Behold the virgin shall conceive and bear a Son and*

*shall call His name Immanuel and the Lord God will
give Him the throne of His father David.* ["12](#)

Luke adds, without hesitation, from the writings
of Samuel:

*"Through Samuel, he spoke to David: When your
days are fulfilled and you rest with your fathers, I
will set up your seed after you who will come from
your body, and I will establish his kingdom. He will
build a house for my name and I will establish the
throne of his kingdom forever.* ["13](#)

This spontaneous exchange continues; Gamaliel adds
from Isaias, looking directly into Mary's eyes, and with
an overwhelming sense of excitement and understanding
he can hardly contain:

*"For unto us a Child is born, unto us a Son is given;
and the government will be upon His shoulder, and
His name will be called Wonderful, Counselor, Mighty
God, Everlasting Father, Prince of Peace.* ["14](#)

This is an extraordinary moment for them. They were
strangers a mere few hours before. Now, they are joined
in a spiritual revelation from the prophesies of their
people concerning Mary's Child that will bond them
together forever.

Joseph comes walking down the grass hillside toward them. As he nears, he also is speaking aloud the continuing words of Isaias that Gamaliel had spoken moments before:

*"And of the increase of His government and peace there will be no end. Upon the throne of David and over His kingdom, to order it and establish it with judgement and justice, From that time forward, even forever. The zeal of the Lord of hosts will perform this."*[15]

Joseph joins them under the tree and sits down.

Mary speaks humbly, showing more understanding of the ancient writings than is customary for the women of those times. "I often think this myself:

*"Nathan the prophet spoke these words to King David, who asked God: "Who am I, O Lord God? And what is my house that you have brought me this far? Let the house of Your servant be blessed forever."*[16]

"Yes," Luke adds. "This is truly why we've come."

Gamaliel is now unabashedly grasping in his thirst for more. "May I ask, Mary, what happened on your return from Elizabeth and Zacharias' house, after John was born?"

"Of course; I hope I am not taking too much of your time," she says respectfully. It is late in the day.

Neither man answers her at first. Glancing over tentatively at Joseph, Luke, changing the question a bit, directs to Mary: "I can't imagine it was easy for you when you returned here," discreetly imploring her to continue, respectfully asking this obviously difficult question in her husband's presence.

"Joseph was outside, working on the house he was preparing for us, when I arrived back in Nazareth," Mary notes. "Even though I knew God would make this right, I was nervous, for sure," she says, glancing at her husband. "I got off the cart, and as I did, my shawl opened slightly, revealing my condition to Joseph. He stood there, stunned," she says.

As she recounts the story, Joseph is stoic and lifts his head slightly, yet manages a slight smile of acknowledgement.

Mary continues: "I walked toward him but couldn't stop. I felt terrible for him in the moment. I walked past him and entered my parents' house. They were both at home. My mother excitedly walked toward me, but swiftly realized from my face that something was wrong. She stopped a step or two from me. I pulled my shawl back with both hands. She looked down and began to cry."

Mary continued, "My father entered from the other side of the room just as Joseph came in the door behind me. I felt trapped. My spirit spoke for me: 'I have my virtue,' I said aloud. 'I have broken no vow, no law of our people.'

"With this, I walked away toward my room, leaving the three of them. I could hear them, and the angst in the room behind me. I believe my father thought that Joseph and I had been with each other before I left. I heard Joseph say, 'You must believe me,' to him."

"This is true," Joseph adds, looking at both men.

He continues, without embarrassment: "I was certainly confused, and admittedly I was in agony. I left the house. I ran until I couldn't run anymore."

Mary, as if feeling her husband's pain all over again, waits, then turns from him to the men: "Over time, my parents believed me, though it certainly sounded impossible. Even now, if I recall it, it all seems like a dream."

Reassured, turning to the men and Joseph still, she adds: "But obviously, it was not."

"Joseph, we know the consequences of such a discovery, what is in our law..." Gamaliel continues.

"How did I keep this from scandal and punishment?" Joseph says, finishing Gamliel's question for him.

Gamaliel nods affirmatively, his eyes never leaving Joseph's.

Glancing over to Mary, Joseph replies: "Well... there were voices seeking punishment, strict adherence to our laws. Mary was steadfast over many days regarding the Child's conception. I spent much time contemplating how to handle this. For some reason, I did not want to hurt her, even if her story turned out to be... different.

"But… I am just a man. I thought to put her away, privately, and without judgment by our elders. I loved her family as well and did not want them to have to bear this embarrassment for the rest of their lives. I was greatly conflicted, to be honest."

Joseph continues: "Then, one night, I was in an extremely restless sleep. I was having bad dreams. I saw her being stoned by my friends and the people of the town. I saw blood and great conflict. I was tormented by thoughts of what would happen to Mary—and to me—should we be accused and found guilty of adultery and fornication before our people.

"I woke up in the middle of the night in a sweat, extremely troubled. I sat up, but was still in a sleep, dazed. Within seconds, I saw my room slowly begin to light up, as if someone with a lamp had entered the room; it began slowly at first, and then I saw a man—an angel, I realized. I don't know how. He was enveloped in light, almost transparently, from behind him, I supposed.

"I did not know if I was awake or still dreaming. He spoke these words to me, though I heard more with my spirit than my ears:

*"Joseph, son of David, do not be afraid to take to you Mary as your wife. For that which is conceived in her is not of any man but is of the Holy Spirit. She will bring forth a Son, and you shall call his name Jesus, Savior, for He will save His people from their sins."[17]*

"As quickly as the angel came, he was gone," Joseph continues. "I awoke from sleep and realized what was happening. My spirit felt free, and I believed."

"I arose and went over to Mary's home, even though it was the middle of the night. I aroused Mary and her parents and told them of the vision. As unbelievable as this all was—visits from angels, conceptions from God—we recalled 'the virgin will be with child' from our sacred writings. We were all there in the middle of the night, filled with certainty and the Lord's peace."

"So, what you did you do formally?" Luke asks.

"What could we do?" Joseph replies. "We believed. I did as the angel commanded me. I took Mary to be my wife in the eyes of all the people."

———

"In days to come," Mary adds, "Joseph and I met with my parents, Anne and Joachim, and determined that I would stay at my parents' house until the marriage ceremony. Joseph continued to build the house he was preparing for us to have a family.

"I worked as much as I could that harvest, being a help to my mother and others. The harvest was unusually abundant that year—figs, almonds, wheat, grapes, pomegranates. The flocks were abundantly increasing as well. God's blessing was on all of Nazareth."

"This was about the time of the census beginning, was it not?" Gamaliel directs to them.

Joseph replies: "One day, soldiers came on horseback to Nazareth, abruptly, intimidating the people with their horses and standards, to collect their taxes. Recognizing the abundance of the harvest and the increase of the people of Nazareth, the soldiers and tax collectors were especially harsh to the people. They were less interested in payments of chickens, grain, and fruits to fill Herod's coffers as they were in gold and a material increase which they were sure the people were hiding.

"Still more soldiers arrived with the decree. It was announced that Caesar Augustus was seeking to honor himself by counting all of his subjects in Galilee, in Judea, and throughout the world, and was going to proclaim a 'great feast.'" Joseph says this somewhat cynically. "Caesar sought to celebrate his 'greatness,' the fact that there was 'peace' in the kingdom."

Joseph adds: "All peoples were going to have to go to their ancestral homelands, where they were to be registered. The people took this to mean more taxes—perhaps to feed Herod's insatiable appetite for his buildings and palaces, we presumed."

Gamaliel raises his eyebrows and looks around, almost as if hiding something, embarrassed, as he is used to appeasing the Romans and the ruling classes and conditioned to temper his inner contempt for them publicly.

Joseph continues: "I, being a descendant of David, had to make the trip a hundred stadia from Nazareth to Bethlehem in Judea to register. Mary had expressed concern at the thought of me having to make the journey alone, let alone at this time. She was nearing the end of her term."

Mary adds: "We went to my family, and it was decided that I had sufficient days until my time to give birth and that I should make the journey with him."

"She is brave, my wife," Joseph adds. "I could not say no, though I knew the journey would be difficult at times. I did try to reason with her to stay here until my return. She seemed to feel some sense of importance to go. So, Joachim insisted we take his beast to help her make the journey as comfortable as possible. We brought as much as we could as well. We left two days later."

With this, Luke's first interview regarding Jesus concluded. With his urging, Mary had begun to relate her story for the ages. She was honest, having no small degree of concern for her visitors, wanting them to be the bearers of the valid word one day.

———

Gamaliel and Luke stayed the night in Nazareth, planning on departing in the morning. They stayed up half the night, pondering what had been told them. They decided among themselves that they would try to delay giving their account to the elders, wanting to, if possible, keep the family from further scrutiny from the authorities.

"I have so many questions still, Luke," Gamaliel noted before falling off to sleep.

"I know," the younger physician added. "Perhaps in the morning."

# Chapter Four
# Gleaning in the Fields of the Lord

---

In the fields outside Bethlehem, the shepherds were quietly moving their flocks.

This small group of men lived a rustic life, one most of them enjoyed. Their freedom, and the peace, appealed to them. The work was steady, albeit that being often outside meant subjection to harsh conditions and long days and nights.

Taking charge of the sheep of Elimelech in town, one of the more wealthy and affluent citizens in Bethlehem, came with both security and risk. Elimelech's flock was enlarging. Wealth was important to him, as it gave him increasing stature in Jerusalem a few miles away, where he traded and often met with the authorities. He was, though, to those who knew him, a patriot of the nation.

Elimelech was a relative of the husband of Naomi, who had died while in Moab with her and their sons. The same Naomi that had returned with Ruth, her daughter-in-law and the Moabitess who had married Boaz, following the time of the famine many centuries earlier. His family had remained one of the prominent families in Bethlehem for hundreds of years.

Elimelech often used the wool of the sheep during shearing to sell to the women in Bethlehem, Jerusalem, and surrounding towns, who in turn used the wool for weaving garments, blankets, and other accessories which they sold in the marketplaces of Jerusalem. It was a lucrative business.

The fields of Judah stood in stark contrast to the barren deserts just a few miles away. There were green pastures in summer, perfect for pasturing sheep, extending for miles in every direction. The sheep naturally trimmed them as they ate the rich, green grass and kept them manageable for miles. The wheat and barley fields grew long and were gold in the time of harvest, dry in winter.

There were harvesters that the people employed during the wheat and barley harvests. Bethlehem's grain was exceptionally robust. The people baked a wide variety of loaves, cakes, and ceremonial offerings from the harvests. They kept and stored much of the grain from a single harvest to last them until the next one. There were vast amounts of it in harvest, so that many enjoyed the benefits both in Bethlehem and in the surrounding villages.

In the town and the surrounding villages, there were several threshing floors and public grinding mills that had been built centuries before, even before the time of Boaz. Ephas of grain were gleaned, shared, sold, and distributed. Bethlehem's fields were indeed abundant. It was no accident that Bethlehem was called "the House of Bread," for so it was.

The fields fed the flocks and the people. The shepherds were able to move the flocks—Elimelech's and others—throughout the fields, the hillsides, and the pastures all the year long. They were a natural resource that had served the people for generations.

On several of the hillsides there were freshwater streams that ran through the base of the hillsides. These streams provided water for the flocks and refreshed the shepherds, who were out in the fields often for days, weeks at a time.

Occasionally, the shepherds were able to take small fish from the streams as well, providing them delicious sustenance for their fires late at night.

There was danger out there as well.

Wolves and wild dogs would occasionally stalk the flocks at night. The shepherds recognized it as an occupational hazard, and more so as their duty to protect every one of the animals. They would often say, "Of our flocks, not a single one of them would be lost."

The shepherds were given written accounts for the flocks they were taking into the fields. "X" many ewes, lambs, goats; at times even noting the spotted animals from those without blemish. They would prove these accounts to Elimelech each time when returning the flock to shelter in the town after its time in the fields.

Elimelech owned land that had a small cave on it, just on the outskirts of town. He had built a small overhang of wood at its entrance to shelter some of the flock and the larger animals during the winter or in bad weather.

A natural rock shelter, it was about forty feet deep, with the low-hanging wooden roof at the entrance, perfect for supporting his flocks. The cave was dry and kept in the heat despite the harsh conditions outside. In winter, the flocks were fed here on the dry sheaves left over from the barley harvests. He had built small watering troughs and hay stands within the cave. He stored the sheaves and excess grain in the cave.

When the shepherds would return Elimelech's flocks to the cave, they would often rest outside it, staying for days at a time, making camp there. Jonathan would slip away, walking stealthily just off the road, making his way to his oft-visited second home in town.

Esther was keenly aware of when the boys were in the town. She would often hastily bake enough loaves for there to be warm bread for Jonathan to take back with him into the fields, for David and the shepherds as well.

On this occasion, as he turned to cross the road in front of Zechariah and Esther's home, playful mischief would enter his little mind. Despite recently promising not to enter through the kitchen window, he couldn't help himself. He loved to surprise Esther. And she loved being surprised by him.

This time, it was he who was going to be surprised.

As he stealthily moved around the house, he saw a small table that was outside the rear of the house at the base of the rear window. He found the window opened a bit. As he lifted himself up, he found the window entry blocked by several potted herbs Esther had evidently placed there for sunlight. He stood there a moment. Suddenly, Esther's face burst through the plants, just a foot or so from his. "Is this my little friend?" she asked abruptly, startling her visitor. "Or has someone come to take my parsley?" she said with a smile.

Jonathan, startled, fell backward off the stool, landing on his buttocks in the dust. Hesitating a second or two and seeing that he wasn't hurt, they both let out hearty laughs, enjoying the moment.

"Come in, dear heart," Esther directed to the boy. "But through the front door!" she said with a mock sternness, with an impish mother's smile.

The wonderful smell of freshly-baked bread filled the house. She kissed the top of Jonathan's head as he entered. "I saw you and your group coming into town this morning," she said. "I thought you all would like some bread to enjoy, Jonathan." The boy smiled and said, "Thank you," though by now, he had come to anticipate his benefactor's graciousness with every visit. He loved to keep up appearances of being surprised to the old lady, as he felt it gave her great joy to know how deeply he appreciated her generosity and concern for him and David.

This time, she loaded the boy up with a large woven sack she filled with such an abundance of loaves that he could hardly carry it. After a short visit, Jonathan proudly swung the sack over his shoulder and proceeded down the road.

"A great harvest," he said, smiling as he looked back at his patron.

"We glean greatly, praise the Lord!" she smiled and said joyously in return.

---

The shepherds were very thankful as they saw the boy approaching them, though this time struggling with the sack. One of the younger shepherds leapt to his feet to help the boy. "Still warm," he commented, as he took the sack from the boy and carried it over to the others.

After the midday meal, they rested. "We're going to take Hezekiah's small flock out for the night," the shepherds' leader spoke. "Some of you can stay here and water Elimelech's animals for the night," he added.

"Can I come?" a small voice rang out. It was David.

"No, you and Jonathan stay here." The elder added, "If you want, you can sleep in the cave after you tend to the yearlings. But no fires! You remember what happened last time," recollecting a near-serious incident in the past.

The young shepherd just put a half-smile on his face, acknowledging the incident.

---

The fields were their life. They gave life to the animals. Their produce provided for the people. As the shepherds sat outside the cave, enjoying Esther's loaves, there was a stillness in the air. Twilight was approaching.

After tending to the flock they had brought in earlier in the day, it was time to prepare for night. Several of the shepherds, including the two young boys, bedded down for the night in Elimelech's cave. It was warm. Their sleep was restful and secure.

Bethlehem was still and quiet. The air was crisp and clear. The sky was ablaze with stars. But like virtually every ancestral town and city in Israel interrupted by Augustus' census, the House of Bread would soon be bursting at its seams.

# Chapter Five
## Journeys

---

No one could remember such clamor and congestion on the roads of Judea and Galilee. Many thousands of people were on the move. Families, couples, the elderly. They were walking, riding on camels and donkeys, and pulling crude carts with supplies and people too weak to make the journey on foot.

On every road and path, Roman soldiers kept a watchful eye. The Roman presence was out in force, keeping the peace, keeping crowds moving. From their perches on horseback and at every crossroads and checkpoint, they were also on the lookout for someone.

Word had spread that He who was to be the long-awaited Messiah in Israel had indeed arrived. The circulating news about some sort of virgin birth in upper Galilee had astounded many. To others, word that Israel's king had come to claim His kingdom left no little fear in the halls of Herod's palace, adding to the stress in the occupying force.

The Romans were not impressed. This "development" gave them more to do, even amidst the already intense activity the census had brought on them.

This situation only furthered the confusion. Was this king supposed to be a grown man? A zealot? A child? Did he have an army, or an alignment with the zealots that would take advantage of the movements caused by Augustus' census?

People were on edge. Requirements that they travel to their ancestral homes to register caused no small disruption in the lives of the people. The people were understandably angry, resentful, and uncertain. Most believed the census disguised a coming imposition of even greater taxes to burden the already heavy-laden citizenry. The resentment was palpable. The soldiers enforced the edict with often harsh—even deadly—consequences.

Small skirmishes were breaking out everywhere. Reports of these heavy-handed treatments by the soldiers were causing many to be overly protective of their families, defensive, and even aggressive themselves toward the Roman army. In several towns and in the outskirts of Judean villages such as Jericho and Hebron, the soldiers had taken to the sword to silence transgressors. More than a few had died along the way.

———

Joseph and Mary had travelled the first ten miles from Nazareth, through Nain and Esdraelon, mostly by day. In several days' time, they had arrived near Mt. Gilboa and the western bank of the upper Jordan River.

Mary believed she had a few months left before she was to deliver. Still, the journey was arduous. The nights were cold, especially in the high country near Gilboa. Each day, as sunset came, Joseph would gather whatever sticks he could to make a fire to warm them during the night. The winds coming off the water would subside. The couple, like others en route here and there, would make a small shelter or find clefts in the rocks to stay the night in during their journey.

There were a handful of families from the region around Nazareth who had set out on their travels around the same time, so for part of the trip, Mary and Joseph travelled in the company of others they knew. Their sacks were filled with dates and figs. They would buy other food and fruits such as small fish, bread, grapes, and oranges from women along the way who would weigh out clusters for the travelers. All in all, the journey, though arduous and long, was not completely uncomfortable.

———

For Melchior, Caspar, and their company, their journey westward was an epic trip through the deserts of Parthia, Media, and the eastern territories. They had set out many months prior, guided by the movements of the "star" they had been observing since its rising.

Their caravan followed the ancient trade routes westward, as most would. Travelling in such a large contingent, there was little danger of running into the bandits and thieves they would undoubtedly encounter along such a long route. The star conjunction they were following continued to lead them westward, so bright at times that the caravans decided to continue their journeys travelling by night.

One day, a messenger arrived from the west. Their counterpart from Egypt was on his way and would be joining them on the quest. Several weeks later, their old friend Balthassar of Alexandria arrived, intersecting their caravan en route. His presence surprised them, as he was known to hate long travel.

"Balthassar, what brings you to this place so far from home?" they asked, tongue in cheek. Balthassar spoke not a word but slowly and dramatically, looking them straight in the eyes, lifted his head and raised his arm toward the night sky. "I trust, the very thing that has brought you on your journeys," Balthassar said, pointing to the conjunction of the stars which was now nearing a position almost directly overhead of them.

The caravans moved off the road to set up their camp for a few days. There was water nearby, an old well from ancient days—an oasis in the midst of the barren, unforgiving desert.

"It is written, gentlemen, *'They shall feed along the roads, neither hunger nor thirst,'*" one of them was heard to say. "Imagine, here in the desert." Balthassar added, as if familiar with the writing:

*"For He who has mercy on them will lead them; as if to green pastures and still waters, even by springs of water He will guide them."[18]*

They looked at each other with a bit of apprehensive curiosity, then all at once they burst out laughing. "You are studying their writings, Balthassar?" one of them said.

"Preparing for this journey," he replied. "At least one of us must!" he said, with fake disdain and a half-smile. They all laughed.

"You are quite the student of the ancient writings, Balthassar. Seriously, from whence did you acquire this knowledge?" one asked.

"In Alexandria, the history of these people is quite well-known," he retorted. "After all, these sons of Abraham, as they have come to be known, were slaves of the Egyptians for many centuries. Their God freed them from Pharoah and performed many mighty works only the God of heaven could perform. He gave them the spoils of Egypt.

"There is a legend that their God guided them on the journey to the land they now possess. It is recorded that He went before them in a pillar of fire by night, and a pillar of smoke by day. Yet, they wandered in the wilderness for forty years."

"Pillars of fire and smoke," they murmured under their breaths, while still listening. "Did not Pharaoh object to this?" one of them asked.

"Yes, vehemently," Balthassar continued. "He pursued them and their leader into the wilderness with all his chariots and warriors. They went the way of the Reed Sea and were blocked from escaping his wrath by it. It is said their leader raised a staff, and the water parted! Their entire nation passed through on dry ground. When the Egyptians followed them, the sea walls crashed down and killed them all. Thus, they proceeded to Canaan."

"These are children's legends, are they not?" one of their wards asked.

"It is further written that this God fought for them against the Canaanites and many other powerful peoples who were in the land," one of them added. "They inherited lands, houses, vineyards, winepresses, and fields already settled. Their ancestors are still there today."

"Children's stories?" one noted. "Is that what we are following?"

As they raised their tents, members of their entourage brought the camels to the troughs near the springs. They, in turn, filled the large, heavy jars and skins for their continuing journey.

As the day fell into night, the sky was ablaze with thousands of stars on the most crystal-clear night in recent memory.

"It is also written that Abraham's children will be as numerous as the stars of heaven," one of them commented, looking up at the vast heavens.

The unusual stars they had each been following were becoming brighter and more visible, even to the untrained eye. Those in their company asked about it, getting little counsel back from the three wise men leading them. As these stars became more and more prominent, it became obvious to their charges that this was somehow tied to their journey.

One night along the way, the conjoining stars were now entering the constellation of Virgo, the virgin. Marveling at this in the early night sky, they all were looking up when a startling point was made—a lone voice against the silence: "A child, in his mother's womb," Balthassar said, as they all looked to each other and nodded their heads in limited but growing understanding.

"Before their journey is finished," Caspar said, "our wanderers will enter Leo. A king, a lion, a leader unlike any other is coming."

That night, the three *magupati* stayed up most of the night as their band slept. "We will be travelling westward, then south," Melchior said confidently.

"The God of heaven is leading us on this journey. No doubt, this is His King we will find."

# Chapter Six
## The Little Drummer Boy

---

*Several Years Earlier:*

It can get very lonely out in the shepherds' fields.

In the fields outside Bethlehem, a rugged band of shepherds tended year-round to the flocks of their patrons, as others had for centuries.

Binyamin was the leader of this small community. He had been a stoneworker until, while working on a spacious home in Bethany in Judea many years before, a wall they were constructing fell, crushing him under several large stones. He had broken his leg severely, such that he was unable to ever work again in this craft.

He had never had a family, per se. Nor anyone to take care of him while he convalesced from his injuries.

Binyamin had travelled throughout the region, picking up small tasks to provide for himself. He worked with wool at table and did some odd handiwork with wood. One day, while working with the shearers in Bethany, he met a woman who asked if he was willing to help in the wool harvest outside of town. He obliged, and for a season or two did light work around their land in exchange for boarding and subsistence.

Over time, he helped the more senior hands feed and move the family's flocks amid the adjacent hills. Binyamin loved the peace and freedom of the outdoors, despite the often-cold nights and the constant vigilance his role as shepherd brought to the work. There were indeed wild animals throughout Judea, and wild and dangerous people as well.

Binyamin never fully recovered from the stone accident. Though he was able to walk, he did so slowly. Gimp, but never in much pain thereafter, he reckoned to lead a simpler life in the fields.

He met Asher from Jericho, and together the two of them led flocks, eventually making their way to the outskirts of ancient Bethlehem of Judea. It was here that the two met Elimelech of Bethlehem.

Over several years, the two shepherds grew their band to a half dozen men. They were quiet men who took pride in their work. Living outside most of the time, they depended on the townspeople from time to time for their generosity and help for the things they needed.

Bethlehem was a small and close-knit community of 300 or so people who knew each other. Many were direct descendants of King David, Ruth, Boaz, and others of renown in this small town, so they were at the same time simple, yet proud of a great heritage.

One day, while in town to take their charge with Elimelech's flock, there was a calamity in a far part of town. Two Bethlehemites who had gone to Jerusalem and the markets there had gotten into an unintended altercation with a vendor. An argument ensued. A man nearby drew a knife and came up behind one of the Bethlehemites. He stabbed him in the side. The Bethlehemite, named Caleb, fell to the ground.

The increasingly tense scene drew two Roman soldiers from their post. Mistaking the second to be the instigator, they drew their swords. One of the soldiers hit the man, causing him to fall in the street, hitting his head. He fell unconscious, and now both men were lying in the streets, dead. A melee ensued, then subsided. Another merchant recognized both of the dead. After speaking at length with the Romans, he volunteered to discreetly take both of the dead men back home to Bethlehem, a journey of about six miles.

The soldiers were all too quick to oblige, hoping to rid themselves of any further inquiry in the bulging, crowded city. The merchant loaded their bodies on his cart and made his way back to the town with haste. Upon arrival, the man found the house of one of the town's elders, a man named Simeon. "Caleb and Ephraim, oh my Lord.

No!" the elder exclaimed. "How did this happen? What has been wrought on us?"

Ephraim was a merchant in the city. Not originally from Bethlehem, he had been a widower for several years since his wife Dina had died in childbirth several years before. Ephraim had two sons who were now suddenly orphans.

By this time, there was no small gathering at the house of Simeon, the people discussing what had happened amongst themselves. One of the townspeople heard that Ephraim's two sons were at play near the caves outside town. He ran in haste and found the children playing with other children from the town. "Come boys, come quickly," the man extolled. "Something has happened."

In the ensuing days, the community sought to take up the longer-term issue of the care of the boys. They had no near-kinsman or relatives here.

"Who will take care of these children?" Simeon asked aloud in an assembly at the synagogue one afternoon.

Elimelech and Binyamin had had a brief conversation about the children as well, following the accident. While gathering Elimelech's flock from his stable cave that day, Binyamin witnessed the townsman gathering the boys. He saw their fear and sadness. It broke his heart that these two young boys were now alone in the world.

"The fields are no place for children," Elimelech retorted sternly to Binyamin. The elder shepherd thought that he could help occupy the boys until suitable accommodations could be made for their care or adoption. "We are right outside of the town," the elder shepherd replied. "They can help us to feed your flock and care for the newborn lambs," he added. "I will see to their needs and safety until you find more permanent care for them."

It was an unusual proposition for sure. Some discussion about the situation had been going on among the people. Zechariah had strongly discerned that perhaps someone from Bethlehem should travel to Zoar, where it was believed Ephraim hailed from. "Perhaps there will be relatives who will care for the boys," Simeon reiterated.

Binyamin was about to leave Bethlehem with the flock when Elimelech came walking briskly down to the stable cave. He had both boys in tow with him. Jonathan was an enthusiastic, resourceful boy of about seven; David, the younger, about five. "Take the boys with you," Elimelech said. "Here is some food and water as well, and some blankets. Keep them safe until your return."

Thus began the journey of Jonathan and David among the shepherds.

No formal adoption was ever affected. It seemed the whole town of Bethlehem adopted them and took an interest in their care. None more than Binyamin and his band of shepherds. In turn, the boys loved Binyamin.

Over several years, the boys grew and lived among the people. They loved the fields and the flocks. They were the joy of the area and knew everyone.

———

Jonathan liked to bang a small drum that one of the older shepherds had made for him—a hollowed-out gourd with a skin stretched over it, tied with a discarded harp string.

He once saw a company of Roman soldiers marching on the outskirts of Bethlehem toward Jerusalem. At the head of the standard bearers, a line of drummers pounded out a steady cadence all the soldiers marched to. When the drummers ceased, the company halted. He was impressed by the discipline of the whole thing and loved the percussion of the drums.

So, Jonathan liked to go ahead of the flock when the shepherds moved them from pasture to pasture. He would slowly, gently hit his drum, which seemed to calm and direct the flock in the direction they wished them to go. He also banged the drum loudly and fearlessly when foxes and other wild animals approached the flock. He believed his drum to have special powers.

One evening, when the shepherds were retiring with the flock, the unmistakable howls of a wolf pack known to the shepherds echoed into their camp. The night was misty from an early evening rain. The flock was stirred and increasingly uneasy.

The red eyes of a wolf could be seen not fifty feet from where the shepherds lay. Two of them leapt to their feet with their staffs to fend off the wolves and pull them farther from the flock. In the hustle that ensued, a lamb sprinted out from the flock, bleating and afraid.

Jonathan ran after it quickly in the dark, all the while hastily hitting the small drum hanging from his belt, believing its magic powers would deter the wolves and save the lamb. The lamb made its way to the rocky slope of a nearby hill, Jonathan and one of the shepherds in quick pursuit, not knowing where the wolves were in the dark. The lamb bleated in distress.

Out of nowhere, young David, who had been awakened by the howling, sprinted with childlike abandon past the two, all the while shouting bravely at the unseen danger, waving a small stick. His little legs propelled him up the slope almost blindly in the dark. He began slipping on the rocks without thought and headed in the direction of the bleating.

David got about twenty feet or so up the slope when he came to a small cliff he could not discern in the dark. The young boy fell headlong onto the rocks below.

"Da...vid...!" Jonathan screamed out. Between Jonathan and the cliff, the wolf emerged. Not ten feet away, Jonathan could see the silhouette of the lamb, caught in a thicket. Jonathan picked up a stone and flung it at the wolf. He scored a direct hit on its forehead. The wolf let out a distressed whimper and sprinted away.

Jonathan inched his way toward the cliff edge, In the faint light, he could see the movement of Binyamin below, picking up the moaning but conscious boy. The child had broken his leg severely. His shin bone was sticking out of the skin, his ankle turned unnaturally to one side. "He's hurt badly," Binyamin exclaimed. "But he's alive."

As one of the older shepherds made his way to the little lamb, he untangled it from the thicket and laid the lamb across his shoulders, carrying it back down to the edge of the field. Jonathan was by now with Binyamin and David. They took the young boy back to their camp.

In haste, Binyamin cleaned the wounds. He gave a small stick to Jonathan. "Have him bite on this," he said, while two shepherds held the boy down. Binyamin proceeded to snap the leg together, aligning the broken bone. The child let out a terrible scream and passed out. Binyamin tied a straight stick together with some cloths all the way from the boy's knee to his ankle to brace the badly broken leg. As David remained semi-conscious and sleeping, the entire band of shepherds stood vigil over the boy.

Jonathan held his brother all night.

---

David awoke a full two days later. He was still in much pain. Some women from the town had arrived with some water and ointment to help dress the wound further. One of them brought along two small crutches for the boy, which she had in the home from an earlier time when her own son had need of them. She had added some clean padding to the tops of the crutches for the boy.

"Do you think he'll ever walk?" the women asked, giving a cup of cold water to the boy.

"We will just have to see," Binyamin replied. "I did," Binyamin added, recalling his own accident.

---

After several weeks, the young boy was up and walking with the crutches. Over time, he would learn to move with them with only slight difficulty, often almost sprinting to keep up with Jonathan and the other shepherds.

Over several years, David grew and stayed with his brother in the care of Binyamin and his company. The boys loved him and the life they had been given. Indeed, most of Bethlehem took pride in the children and watched out for them, providing for their needs as often as possible.

Jonathan and David were inseparable.

When the company moved, the littlest shepherd with the mangled leg would be seen determinedly keeping up with the other shepherds and the flocks. By now, he carried a slingshot at his side, along with a stick he used to direct the sheep as they moved. But it was the steady beat of his brother's drum that would give him the cadence to walk tall every day.

## Chapter Seven
# The Stem of Jesse

—

Many fires were burning, illuminating the town. Torches lined the streets and pathways to give light to them. The glow of the menorahs could be seen inside each of the houses.

Several houses displayed larger instruments at front doors, outside the homes, further illuminating the darkened streets.

The night was clear and full of stars.

Shortly before sunset, a number of the men gathered at the synagogue for evening prayers. Zechariah led them in reading from the ancient scrolls the stories of the victories of David, of the people and God's providence in ancient times, the assault that led to Judah Maccabee's victory, and the celebrations Bethlehem was commemorating this night.

"We are David's people," Zechariah exclaimed. "We are of the root and stem of Jesse, as God had promised long ago."

"Praise be to His holy name," the men chanted in reply:

*"Barukh attah Adonai Eloheinu Melekh ha-olam, asher kideshanu bemitzvotav vetzivanu lehadlik ner shel chanukah."*

*"Blessed art thou, Lord our God, King of the universe, who sanctifies us with Thy commandments and commands us to kindle the light of Channukah."*

The lights of Bethlehem were everywhere. Not only here in this little town, but throughout the country—in Jerusalem, in Galilee, and throughout all of Judea—the people lit their candles, their lamps, their menorahs and torches, and celebrated this Festival of Light.

Despite the Romans being stationed in every town and village, this night, there was peace. Saturnalia brought with it a certain bit of celebration, of drunkenness in its own celebration, which ultimately distracted most of the revelrous soldiers.

The emperor was certainly to be appeased, and his legions only too willing to oblige. The celebrations of Saturnalia and Pater Patriae existed side by side this season. And the Jews celebrated their own Feast of Light.

In the town square, the people made their way in. Tables had been set up wherein several types of breads, *sufganiyot*, and sweets were being served by the towns-women. Stalks of dry wheat and stems of palms were adorned with bangles and dressed the gathering place.

Esther was there. Children played games. Players played, and some of the people danced into the night.

As the night wore on, even the children stayed up celebrating. In the center of the square, all the people began to gather in circles, surrounding a small seat of hemp and hay. Two of the townspeople escorted a young blind woman to the seat. Her name was Rachel. She had been blind from birth. Everyone in the town looked forward to times when Rachel would sing.

Though blind, Rachel played the harp. Like her ancestor David, she would sing the joys of God's faithfulness and lament the days of hope lost or delayed. She knew David's psalms and those of Moses, Asaph, and Solomon, and the contemplations of Heman and Ethan.

The crowd fell silent. Rachel put her fingers to the strings of the harp and plucked a string, then another, then ever so gently ran her fingers across them all. The gentle sound resonated throughout the square, the people silent and attentive to her prelude.

*"My heart is steadfast, oh, oh, God,"* she sang angelically. *"I will sing to You and give You praise. Awake… my glory! Awake… lute and harp. I… will awaken the dawn."*

The people sat joyfully still as Rachel sang. The night was crisp and bright. The fires and torches lent a slight breeze of warmth to the gathered crowd. No one seemed to mind the cool.

As mothers held their children and fathers lifted theirs on their shoulders, the air was filled with Rachel's praise:

*"I… will praise You, oh Lord… among the peoples; I will sing to You among the nations. For Your mercy…*

*reaches unto the heavens, and Your truth… unto the clouds."*

Then again:

*"Be exalted, O God, above the heavens; let Your glory be… above all the earth."*

A stillness remained on the inspired throng as Rachel ended her songs of praise. Rachel, as if in a trance, let out a drawn-out breath and lowered her harp. She smiled angelically to those gathered. The people let out strains of appreciation that filled the square.

Zechariah stepped forward and spoke aloud to the people:

"Children of Bethlehem! To you it was written by Isaias the prophet, long ago:

*"There shall come forth a Rod from the stem of Jesse, and a Branch shall grow out of his roots. The Spirit of the Lord shall rest upon Him, the Spirit of wisdom and understanding, the Spirit of counsel and of might, the Spirit of knowledge and of the fear of the Lord."[19]*

*"He will judge for the poor and decide with equity for the meek of earth. This Root shall stand as a banner to all people; the Gentiles will even seek him! And His resting place will be glorious."*

Zechariah slowly lowered his outstretched arms, his hands still lifted to heaven. A slight breeze came across the square. The night was brilliant, the sky filled with stars.

Quietly, the people arose and began to disperse. Several stopped at Rachel to greet her, still sitting in the midst of the departing crowd.

"Thank you, daughter," an older woman exclaimed gently. "Bless you, Rachel, and your voice," another added. "You will surely harken the Messiah when He comes to visit us, His people!"

Rachel simply smiled in humble acknowledgement. Surely He was to come to the people one day, she thought.

———

Several miles outside town, Joseph and Mary had bedded down to rest for the night. They could see the distant fires of Jericho and Bethabara, glistening in the still of the night.

"We should reach Bethlehem in a day or so," Joseph said to Mary, his quiet voice interrupting the stillness of the breeze.

She looked at the star over her head and stared at it for many minutes. She felt the Child within her stirring. She gently placed her hand on her stomach. The Child calmed and was at rest once again.

As Bethlehem slept, Mary simply smiled and closed her eyes. On the morrow they would reach their destination. She drew herself closer to the fire, and to Joseph.

# Chapter Eight
## Do Not Be Afraid: Zechariah's Song

The morning sun was glorious the day after the festival in Bethlehem. An unusually large, white-orange sun rose slowly and majestically over the distant hills. Only a handful of people were up and stirring, some cleaning up fragments of bread and festival props left in the streets from the night before.

Zechariah loved this time of morning. He often walked quietly to the edge of the village to commune with God in silence before the day's work. This day, he took a seat on a small outcropping behind Elimelech's cave that protruded out as a natural platform, facing the fields. Here, he greeted the sun and spoke to God.

"Ancient of Days, Jehovah our Deliverer, my Lord of lords, we yearn for you," Zechariah prayed, halfway between silent meditation and whispers aloud of a heart at peace.

"You renew Your promises each morning. You ride the wings of the wind and swiftly bring the hope of a new day to Your people. I praise You greatly, dear Lord."

Zechariah often believed his prayers would ride the wind to the distant hills and land at the feet of God. He very often prayed for the people.

He prayed for his family. He prayed for the peace of Israel and their release from the Roman oppressors. This day, he was contemplating an uneasiness he felt despite the celebrations of the night before. He couldn't place the source of this uncertainty and asked God to give him peace.

At times, he heard the voice of the Lord in reply. He had hoped today would be one of those days.

In his spirit, he groaned. "Yahweh, You have shown us that You deliver Your people. Who is like our Lord, that You ransom us? You parted the seas to give us exit from bondage in Egypt. Miriam, Moses, and Aaron and all the people saw Your great hand. They danced with timbrel and tambourine on the bodies of their enemies. You flung every one of our enemies into the sea. And who are we Ephrathites, dear God, that You have built us on so sure a foundation?" He pondered Bethlehem's past and continued, now with hands upstretched to the heavens beyond the hills.

"You gave us Rachel, our mother; Naomi and Ruth, our sisters; Boaz, Jesse, and our forefathers. We are the descendants of David, Your anointed. You made the smallest among us to be king over the nation. Among all the princes and tribes of Israel, You have shown Your favor on us, Your people."

His prayers turned to the occupation, and the true freedom which eluded them.

"Though the evil one come against us, Lord, we shall not be afraid, for You are with us. Your rod and your staff, they comfort us. For it is written, *'We shall fear no evil.'* Of whom shall we be afraid, Lord? As You did with David, our father, You have anointed our heads with oil; our cup overflows.

"You are among us, O Lord."

Zechariah pondered what his spirit had just uttered. He paused in silent elation and put his head down.

———

Several miles away, Joseph and Mary were greeting the dawn, albeit much more slowly, after the long night. Joseph stoked a small fire to give Mary some warmth before continuing their journey.

A small stream ran through the field they had rested in overnight. After rinsing off some evening cloths and a small towel, Joseph took a skin and proceeded down the dew-borne hillside to the brook. He walked into the crisp, clear stream and washed himself. When finished, he filled the skin for Mary and their journey and walked back up the small hill.

Mary seemed uncomfortable. She did not complain, but as she stood, she placed both her hands on her hips and bent forward.

Suddenly, the clatter of several horses broke the stillness, and a small band of soldiers rode by in a gallop, never even slowing to glance at the couple in the grass.

Mary looked up, silently.

"Don't be afraid, Mary," Joseph told her. "We are almost there. They will not harm us," he said, seemingly reassuring himself as well.

The journey from Nazareth had been perilous at times. Soldiers were frequently stopping pilgrims and interrogating them, often aggressively, extorting something from them as the price of being allowed to continue on to their ancestral homes.

Uneasiness broke the journey's peace and tranquil landscapes. They were tired, hungry. And Mary was quietly beginning to experience labor pains, despite being still weeks from her time for birth.

Concurrently, several miles away, Zechariah was deeper in prayer. He was deeply meditating on his own words which had struck his spirit:

"You are among us, O Lord."

His people had waited generations—millennia—for God's presence to be fully revealed to them. Through times of strife and distance, times of rebellion—even idolatry—when they forgot the Lord their God, God never forgot them.

Sitting on that outcropping at the edge of the fields, the words of Habakkuk—one of the lesser prophets of generations before—came to his spirit:

*"For even if the fig tree does not blossom, nor fruit be on the vines; though the olives fail and the fields yield no food; even if the flocks be cut off from the fold and there be no herds in the stalls, Yet will I rejoice in the Lord. I will joy in the God of my salvation."*[20]

Zechariah never wavered in his faith. This day, something else was in him.

The stillness was broken only slightly. At the outcropping in Bethlehem, from a distance, could be seen a small band of the shepherds, bringing two sheep back to Elimelech's cave. A mother and her lamb.

"Peace be with you, Zechariah," one of the shepherds said softly as they neared.

Zechariah was deep in the spirit. He only lifted his head slightly from prayer and without stopping, mustered an: "And to you," said softly.

He put his head back in his hands and continued searching his spirit for several hours before making his way home. He was sure God was speaking back to him, giving him the peace he sought. And he was no longer afraid.

# Chapter Nine
## A Stir in Jerusalem

Peace was not a virtue found often in Jerusalem. This seat of the nation was also the hotbed of rebellion. Mercenaries and zealots often organized and hid outside the city in the caves and deserts of the region to exact their merciless vengeance on their captors.

There was no shortage of so-called leaders of these rebels. They had a system of covert sympathizers throughout the city who provided information on the movement of soldiers, as well as an ample stream of food and supplies with which to supply their rebels.

These men were resourceful. They had access to metals like iron and an expertise in smelting. Underground, they built productive operations, smelting swords and other implements of conflict and revolt. With an increasing supply of young zealots impatient with the demands and burdens of Rome, from these outposts they would frequently launch their guerilla strikes at the Romans, often decimating complete garrisons of arriving soldiers coming to reinforce the troops already there.

The Romans were led by ruthless men themselves—procurators, administrators, mostly the puppets of Rome tasked with enforcing and keeping Rome's version of peace in this desert outpost. It was a most miserable existence; the dust and desert heat were not suitable for any life, even for Rome's soldiers. They resented these "traitors" and sought every opportunity to exterminate them.

One Herod the Great, a Bedouin, had been installed by Rome to rule over what they saw as his people. He taxed the people to build great palaces by the sea in Tyre, within Jerusalem, and in the desert, overlooking the Dead Sea on the formidable, unscalable outpost of Masada.

He also built—rebuilt—the great temple at Jerusalem for the people, their greatest source of national pride and the center of their faith. He built aqueducts, public pools, squares, and gathering places that the people utilized. This kept their hatred of him at bay, at least at times.

Herod, in his self-deceptive pride, believed himself to be loved by the people. This could not have been less true.

Herod was an absolute tyrant. Because of his Roman installation, he was also often called by the ruling priestly class to do their bidding. Their arrangement was, at least, tentative. The priests abhorred him. His renowned lusts for sex, orgies, lavish banquets, and entertainment were legendary. During these "parties," he entertained his officers, cohorts, and a bevy of Roman military who dined and delighted in the delicacies he provided.

This year, Herod had stayed in Jerusalem for Saturnalia and Channukah. His celebrations of the season were decadent, satisfying to the Romans most of all, even at so solemn a feast for his own people.

On this particular day, the refuse from the debauchery the night before was still strewn across the palace banquet halls. Many an unsavory woman who had been invited to the feasts was still present. Despite the gorging and decadence, preparations were being made for yet another night of excess.

There had been violence in the streets the night before. Soldiers had intercepted a wagon filled with swords and knives that was being delivered to the red quarter, the wagon disguised as a vegetable cart selling its wares to the poor. The two men leading the cart had attempted to fight back once discovered. No small incident took place.

Three of Herod's soldiers from the palace, walking nearby, as well as several Roman soldiers, were killed with the sword by the rebels. The rebels seemed to get away but were discovered hiding in the house of a rebel sympathizer some hours later. They were summarily executed on the spot by the soldiers, to the horror of the many gathered curiously to see the disturbance.

There had been an unusually loud celebration of Saturnalia that night by the Roman soldiers. There was pent-up frustration at the constant skirmishes, the overwhelming number of people in the city for Channukah, and the additional demands of the census there. Their leaders had given many of them a night's pass to celebrate and release their inner demons.

It being an extremely clear night, except for the smoke of torches and lamps obscuring parts of the city, the stars were like a "sea of stars," as one would recount at the feast at Herod's palace.

The newest and brightest "star" which had been moving across the eastern sky was now exceedingly bright and brilliant. The people saw it. Several of Herod's distinguished guests stood outside on the palace veranda, observing it and discussing among themselves its unusualness. Few, though, had any concern or really wondered what it was, or what it might portend.

The conjunction that was creating the star appeared to be slowing down in the sky, hovering just south of the city. Some learned scribes and those in Herod's company brought this to Herod's attention, though from the palace portico he had been observing this unusual phenomenon himself for several weeks now.

During the rising of these stars, he had privately inquired of the astrologers. Though he was given their technical observations regarding planets, stars, constellations, and movements, none of the house seers saw anything unusual in this. It was easy for them to chalk these movements up for Augustus. After all, Herod would reluctantly accept these causes at this time.

And they would keep their heads, acknowledging the emperor's omnipotence rather than publicly—or privately—casting doubt on it.

Herod participated in the festivities with a characteristically deceptive outward appearance, though with his characteristic jealousy and brewing wrath, he couldn't hide his inner turmoil from those who knew him best.

A master of investigation and inquiry, he was also hearing a stirring among the people regarding this being the time for God Himself to send a Deliverer. This gave him a degree of anxiety that had changed his behavior at times. For sure, Rome would hold him responsible for keeping the peace—especially during this time of Augustus' proclamations. But his sixth sense told him that this "stirring" of the people was something quite out of the ordinary. There were simply too many taletellers, seeking to earn the king's favor by being the first to bring him such news.

Earlier that day, Herod had occasion to visit at the palace with Nicodemus, one of the rising and most respected pharisees. It was Nicodemus who brought up the stars he himself had been observing. For, acquainted with the well-known wrath of Herod, he had sought to ascertain for himself what might portend from Herod if the stirring of the people persisted. He attempted to distract Herod from his growing wrath.

"I'm sure these are natural to the heavens," he sought to assure the king. "The emperor has brought peace, albeit by the sword. No force will rise against him, Herod."

"And to my kingdom, most revered Nicodemus?" the king asked.

Nicodemus answered him: "As the learned Gamaliel has often said, most excellent Herod, there have been many who came in the name of this one or that one. They have all come to naught."

Herod put aside his anxious thoughts, for the moment. But they would linger. Despite these encouragements from the learned, he had to suffer a constant flow of his own doing, spies bringing him more and more information from the streets. He was consumed with the star, and it twisted him in his own mind.

---

The feast that night was exceptionally decadent, even by Herod's standards. It was as if he was trying to earn the loyalty of soldiers and commanders to ease his insecurities relating to his own throne. He had harlots serve the guests wild game and exotic meats while completely naked, or adorned with large and colorful snakes around their necks. He surprised his guests with contests and games of chance, whereby they would be rewarded with every lustful encounter they could imagine.

Many of these acts took place in full view of those gathered, and for Herod's sinful, satiating entertainment.

Men were brought in to fight unto the death. Musicians were violently taken out and cast into prisons below the palace for playing too loudly or mistakenly making a noise during his frequent pontifications. Wine flowed and flowed, well into the evening and the early morning.

As Jerusalem awoke the next morning, the circle of confusion and fear increased. In the streets, many murmured tales from the palace. Avenues in and out of the city were becoming more and more lined with makeshift crosses, carrying on them the dead or dying bodies of rebels and ordinary citizens caught up in Herod's campaign of chaos and fear. This parade of death extended well beyond the city walls to the roads beyond the city.

The wrath ratcheted up—even during this time of celebration—as under Herod's orders, bands of soldiers barged into houses supposed to be hiding more and more rebels, or this leader he feared worse.

Herod could not sleep. Paranoia fed his anger and unrest. Arrests led to interrogations, which led to few releases, but even more hastily run trials and even on-the-spot executions. Herod's stress was the people's stress. And there was no relief.

As time went on, Herod sensed his rule was being threatened. He couldn't know where it was coming from, but he was determined to crush it.

His fury was burning irrationally. It was only a matter of time before he would unleash terror on the general populace—and their children, worst of all.

# Chapter Ten
## 'Twas the Night Before...

It is early morning of the third day since the festival began. The newly rising sun is illuminating this still-sleeping little village. As shadows progress, people emerge from their homes to begin the business of the day.

Atop a nearby hillside, the silhouette of a slow-moving donkey is seen, its rider atop the beast, is being guided by an obviously tired man walking alongside, leading the beast. They are alone on the road.

The woman atop the animal is obviously in some discomfort.

"Joseph, have we long?" she asks.

"It's atop the next hill," he replies. "We're almost there."

As they near the bottom of the dirt path, their path levels. They see, resting in the fields, a number of people and families, perhaps without lodging and in Bethlehem for the census, or Channukah. They can see up ahead the faint images of two soldiers, Romans, at the gate of the city. As they approach, the soldiers—a bit irritable from perhaps a lack of sleep the night before and being at their positions early in the morning—bid them come closer.

"Come on, come on; you're our first customers of the day."

Joseph approaches the makeshift table they've set up.

"Name?" one of the soldiers asks.

"Joseph bar Jacob," Joseph replies.

"Town?" the soldier continues, obviously a bit aggravated at the monotonous questioning he will undoubtedly repeat many times throughout this day.

"Nazareth of Galilee," Joseph replies.

"This your city?" the soldier asks.

"Yes, my ancestral home. We live in Nazareth," Joseph replies.

"Does anything good come from Nazareth?" one of the soldiers murmurs to the other. They enjoy a demeaning, short laugh.

At first, the soldiers do not pay any attention to Mary on the donkey behind Joseph. The soldier picks up a quill and begins to register Joseph for Caesar Augustus' census.

"The woman with you?" he asks.

"Yes," Joseph responds, "my wife."

Both soldiers take note of Mary, trying bravely to mask her condition and her discomfort. They look down and see that she is visibly with child.

The first soldier looks back over in Joseph's direction and makes another annotation in the registry. "Another subject for Herod," he says out loud, to no one in particular.

"Where will you be staying?" the soldier asks.

"With my relatives, just up the hill," Joseph answers, as Mary winces from a sudden pain.

"Good luck," the soldier mentions cynically, perhaps forgetting to ask the name of their relatives. "There isn't room for a dog in this town right now. Move on," he commands, with a simple wave of his hand and with little compassion for them. He makes no further eye contact with either of them.

As the couple enters the city gate, they see a couple of women drawing water from the ancient well at the gate of the city. It is the same well that David's mighty men came to, to draw water for their future king, centuries before. Joseph pulls the donkey to the side and waits patiently for the women to fill their jars.

One of the women glances over and sees Mary atop the beast and struggling against the continuing, early pangs of childbirth. Her labor pains are unexpectedly growing in intensity and becoming more frequent.

Without a word, the woman smiles at Joseph and hands him a cup of the cold well water for Mary. Joseph humbly returns the smile and hands it to Mary, who smiles, tiredly but glowingly, at the woman. She drinks the cup and hands it back to Joseph without speaking.

The women both smile at each other without speaking a word. They obviously are contemplating what this poor woman atop the beast is going to do in this condition.

"Does she have relatives here to stay with?" one of the women asks softly. At once, completing their draw, they leave the well.

Joseph takes the time to give some water to the donkey and a short cup for himself before filling a skin and hanging it off the back of the donkey. Rinsing the desert dust off their parched mouths, they continue up the hill into the village.

---

Upon arriving at the home of their family with whom he intends them to stay, Joseph ties the beast just outside their modest home and proceeds to walk up the few stairs to the house. He stops only long enough to bless himself at the door. He looks back at Mary for a moment, then peers back into the doorway.

"Peace be upon this house," he speaks. A woman kneading bread in the small room on the lower floor recognizes him.

"Joseph, come; come in."

"Hello, Miriam," Joseph responds, as the two embrace. He glances across the small room. "Where is Eleazar?" he asks. Eleazar is the brother of Joseph's father, Jacob, hence Joseph's uncle.

"He will be right back," Miriam replies. "With so many here for the census, we keep running out of barley.

He went down to the pile at the threshing floor. I've been baking all day for a week now," she says with a smile.

"The town looks full," he replies. "Many in the fields as we neared town, I see," Joseph says.

"Yes," Miriam replies, "some of our family as well. There is not even room at Caleb's rooming house. Too many at one time. But we'll do. Joseph, bring your new bride in," Miriam directs to him with a reassuring smile. "You must be tired. Eat with us and rest a while."

"Thank you," he humbly replies.

Upon exiting the house, he sees Mary standing next to the donkey. "It feels better this way," she claims to Joseph.

"Come, Mary; Miriam is home," he replies.

Miriam is meeting Joseph's betrothed for the first time.

"Welcome to Bethlehem," she says to Mary with a wistful smile, as Mary enters. "And welcome to our home, Mary. You must be tired, child. Here, sit," directing Mary to a cushion in the corner of the room. Mary smiles.

"Mary, how was your journey?" Miriam continues. "You are a brave girl to make such a trip at this time."

Miriam makes no mention of Mary's pregnancy.

Miriam knows of Joseph's betrothal to a young maiden who, travelers have said, was found with child before they were married. She is aware that her nephew did not put his betrothed wife away but plans to raise the Child. Nothing else is said.

"Joseph took good care of us," Mary returns appreciatively. Joseph acknowledges her compliment and simply looks down.

It is morning. As Miriam continues to bake her barley loaves, Eleazar arrives with Joseph's cousin Bartholomew, a young man about Joseph's age. "Cousin!" Bartholomew exclaims upon entering. He hastens over to Joseph and embraces him by both arms extended between each other. "Is life treating you well?" he says, only a foot or so away from his cousin's face. "It must be; we hear you're building a mansion for this new family of yours." All share a bit of a proud chuckle.

"A simple abode," Joseph acknowledges, "if I can ever finish it."

They all have a moment of familial joy at the arrival of Joseph and Mary.

"Augustus would have you do otherwise, my nephew," states Eleazar, in obvious reference to the harsh new taxes that will surely come from the census. He moves toward Joseph and embraces him as Bartholomew steps politely aside. "How is everyone, Joseph?" the elder uncle asks.

"They are well, Uncle," Joseph answers. "They send their regards."

"I am certain they have worried about you on this trip," Eleazar responds, glancing over and smiling at Mary. "And how are you feeling, my dear?"

Mary smiles and tilts her head in acknowledgement.

"Mary, I knew your mother and father when we were young. Are they well?"

"Yes, Eleazar, they are well," Mary responds. "I'm sure they are worrying about us about now."

"Well, there are caravans moving about and many people coming to and fro," the elder adds. "This census has only increased travel. I'm sure we can get word to them that you have arrived safely."

Mary nods appreciatively.

"How was the journey, Joseph?" Eleazar asks.

"There are many people travelling," Joseph responds. "The roads are clogged; many people, like us, are sleeping in the fields along the way."

The older man listens intently, concerned. Joseph continues: "Mary made the journey because we believed the days to her delivery were greater than those of the journey. I am certain it was more difficult than she has confessed," he says with a slight smile, directing his gaze to his wife.

Mary distracts herself from her obvious pain but for a moment to manage an acknowledgement.

"You must have been travelling for over a week, Joseph," Eleazar says. "You must have seen many soldiers."

"We did, Uncle. They seem very tense and impatient. We took the old road through Galilee past Esdraelon. There seem to be stops there that are creating difficulties for the people. Many are being interrogated.

There are confrontations," Joseph says, appearing somewhat relieved that his and Mary's journey is over.

He adds: "After Mt. Gilboa, we stayed along the Jordan to Jericho. The roads are rocky and hilly. I tried the best I could to avoid the hills—and the Romans."

"Let me get you some water and cloths to clean the desert off you, nephew," Eleazar states. "Miriam will bring you some food as well. Come, Mary; rest a while in the upper room here. You will find it a bit quieter before Jacob, Johannes, and their families arrive."

Mary is glad to have a place to rest, and some food. She is becoming more and more uncomfortable, unexpectedly closer and closer to childbirth than either she or Joseph have expected. Perhaps it is the arduous journey, or the difficulty of the mountain roads that have caused her some discomfort that could be hastening her labor.

As Mary settles in the upper room, Joseph leaves her to rest awhile. He goes outside to tend to their animal. He is obviously a bit exhausted from the journey as well, so Joseph goes to the well at the gate and fills several skins to wash him down and water him. Bartholomew brings some hay, from the lower room of the house where Eleazar's animals lay, as well. Joseph rests for a while in the midday heat, falling away gently into an anxious but peaceful rest.

The day progresses. As Joseph checks in on Mary, it becomes apparent that Mary is going to deliver before they depart back for Nazareth. Having overheard that Eleazar's family is arriving soon, and while the beast rests, Joseph stirs himself to walk down the now busy road in the town toward Caleb's inn, where he seeks to arrange shelter and perhaps privacy for Mary.

Caleb is a distant relative on Joseph's father's side. He has not seen him in many years. As Joseph nears the inn, he observes so many people that a number of them are sitting in small groups in the dusty streets opposite the front door. This concerns Joseph. He knocks at the door. An obviously frustrated voice beckons him to enter.

At the same moment, the door opens, and two children race out. With the door partly open, Joseph peers in to see Caleb and a woman carrying linens to others sitting in makeshift spaces. The inn is overflowing with families, children—mostly travelers.

"Joseph, is that you?" Caleb asks, handing some blankets and pillows to a woman and her small family.

"Hello, Caleb," he answers. "I hope you are well."

"Well?" Caleb retorts, somewhat indignantly. "I can barely sleep, let alone provide for all of these people here. You are here for the census, Joseph?"

"Yes," Joseph replies.

He continues, "I was hoping…" but before he can get the sentence out, he is abruptly interrupted by Caleb.

"Joseph, I would love to help you, but I have no room at all, not even on the roof. If you had arrived several days ago, perhaps, but…"

Joseph interrupts him with a growing sense of urgency in his voice, "I understand, Caleb. It's for my wife; she has joined me on the journey from Nazareth, as we thought we had enough time to…"

"Enough time to what, Joseph?" Caleb interrupts. "Did you not believe this town would overflow? David's descendants, Joseph—we are many."

"Mary is with child," Joseph simply answers.

Bartholomew enters and greets Caleb familiarly, stopping at Joseph and whispering discreetly to him: "Joseph, Mary is near."

Joseph stands frozen, paralyzed for a moment, concerned for Mary and needing to get back to her, but realizing he is unable to find space for them.

"I hope I have not brought you any problems, Caleb," Joseph says apologetically.

As he turns to leave with Bartholomew, Caleb comes walking over to him, having heard the whisper. "I am embarrassed, Joseph, but no one is going to have any room, let alone privacy," Caleb states.

He walks out the door with them and, speaking softly so as not to be heard by others in the street, gestures with his hand down the road.

"Joseph, I have a space I rent out at times down at the edge of town. It is not a room, but it is dry. You may find comfort and shelter there."

Bartholomew looks in the direction of Caleb's gesture, a bit confused, looking back at the men, unsure of where or to what Caleb is referring.

With an immediate glimmer of hope, and without hesitation, Joseph says, "Thank you for your kindness; where is it, Caleb?"

"At the end of this road, go down the hill," Caleb says. "You will see a shed protruding from a cave. Shepherds sometimes stay there. Stay there for the night."

Joseph does not hesitate at the thought of staying the night in a cave. He hastens to return to the house of Eleazar. He enters and finds his cousins Jacob and Johannes and their children outside. Their wives are upstairs with Mary.

Upon climbing the several steps to the upper room, he finds Mary unexpectedly sitting up, smiling, and speaking with them. "She is a trooper," Miriam adds with a smile.

Joseph manages a concerned smile back. "Thank you, Miriam, for your hospitality," he answers. "Caleb has given us use of a space for the night. Come, Mary; let us get settled there."

Miriam knows the space Caleb has offered, as many have used it from time to time to store things, and even bed down or shelter their animals when storms came.

Concerned, she says, "Go, Mary. I will bring you some blankets and cloths."

With haste, Joseph and Mary take hold of their animal and proceed down the road to the manger stable Caleb has provided. They find it at the bottom of the grassy hill, as Caleb had said. Joseph ties the animal up and enters it.

The cave is indeed a small rock enclosure, about forty feet deep and twenty-five or so feet wide. As Caleb mentioned, there is a wooden roof or shed covering protruding from the entrance of the cave for shelter from the rain, which makes it resemble a small house of sorts.

Joseph stands staring at it for a few moments. "Our beautiful guest house, Mary," he says, without betraying his inner thoughts at the austere stable.

Mary simply manages a smile and says: "A craftsman's home, Joseph. I'm grateful."

The cave is indeed warm and dry, and relatively clean. There is hay everywhere, covering the floor, even stacked in a small wooden manger which is there for the feeding of sheep. There are also several bundles of barley from the last harvest stacked neatly against the left-side wall of the cave. Inside, there are several animals lying down, seemingly unmoved at the intrusion of people into the manger. A young milk cow, a sheep, a lamb. Mary smiles in the direction of the animals, bemused, perhaps considering this all as Joseph stands inside the cave, looking a bit perplexed himself.

A large water jar is in the front corner, as well as a trough for watering the animals that stands on the right side of the cave, half full.

"Thank you, Joseph, for finding us some shelter," Mary says, with humble sincerity, and to distract Joseph from his obvious frustration. "We haven't had a roof over our head for over a week," she smiles.

Whatever is on Joseph's mind, standing there, he no longer entertains the thought of complaining or making excuses, but goes about the business of setting up some comfort for him and Mary.

———

Joseph chooses a spot in the farthest part of the cave. He brings the animal in and begins to unload everything they have brought along with them for the journey. He gathers straw and packs it down together until it becomes a soft, thick bed for Mary. He places a blanket they have brought over the top of it and steps gently on it to compress it in place. He places a pillow at the head of the makeshift bed and gathers a blue blanket they have carried at the foot of the bed.

Mary sits, pleased, all the while holding the small lamb on her lap, stroking its soft white fur. The little lamb rests its head on her leg. For a moment, she does not feel any pain.

Miriam arrives, carrying some cloths, a blanket, and a jar of cool water, along with some bread and a small clay pot with bit of barley and lentil porridge she has made for her family. "Mary, I will come back a little later," she exclaims. "Joseph, we'll check in with you and see what else you need."

As the day wears on, Joseph sits with his wife. Her pains return. She will later say that they were not harsh at all. The young woman just breathes and prays under her breath, not complaining, all the while knowing that the time for her Child to be born is upon them.

---

As night falls, Mary's labor grows increasingly frequent. Miriam indeed returns to check on her, this time with the two ladies Joseph and Mary had seen earlier that day at the well. The two women carry a large jar of warmed water and cloths.

"Joseph," Miriam directs to him. "Tamara and Bilhah would like to help Mary in her delivery. We are willing to stay here with her." Mary is uncomfortable but dealing with her pain.

"Thank you, sisters; your kindness is appreciated," Joseph replies. Mary smiles in acknowledgement.

"We don't know how long this will last," Joseph adds. "You have done much for us. We will stay here and see how this goes tonight. I will call on you if she is in great distress."

This seems reasonable, acceptable to the ladies and to Mary, who is appreciative of the cloths and warm water. With this, the women return to their homes. Mary speaks not, but continues in what appears to be soft prayers and contemplation amidst real and intermittent labor pains. Joseph observes that, at times, it appears as if she is speaking to someone—someone in the manger with them, someone he himself cannot see. Still, once in a while he turns to check for himself.

Joseph and Mary spend the approaching night comforting each other, speaking of their journey, and remembering the angels that had spoken to both of them months earlier. They pass the time with these recollections of the extraordinary events that have happened to them both. They cannot fully understand what is happening. But it is happening, just as they had been told.

Mary's labor increases in frequency and then lets up for a time. Both Mary and Joseph are preparing for the time of her delivery, which they now believe is imminent.

Through the entrance to the cave, they can see the unusual glow from the light of the star, the same star that had captured Mary's attention the few nights before. The star has grown increasingly bright in the night sky. It is obvious, extraordinary.

They know it is gently, majestically signaling their Child's birth. This both comforts and humbles them.

The couple can hear the occasional commotion outside the cave: the sounds of soldiers in town loudly celebrating Saturnalia this night, and the hustle and bustle of the people. As the night goes on, the sounds of debauchery gradually disappear, until the night becomes completely silent.

In the cool of the crisp, clear night, Mary and Joseph wait, alone in the manger, for Mary to deliver her Child. Around them, the small band of animals stirs, their glad company.

Heaven itself is about to visit its glory on the world, a star lighting the way.

## Chapter Eleven
# The Song of the Hills

––––––

The night grew increasingly crisp and quiet. Unusually quiet—an almost silent night, the older shepherds observed. The night being cold, several of the shepherds had made fires to warm themselves.

Binyamin and Asher were awake, watching the flocks. As the night wore on, a number of the shepherds had lain down to sleep for the night. It was, for all intents, a peaceful night, the men warmed by the fires.

David could not sleep. The littlest of the shepherds, he got up several times to feed the fires. It was after midnight when David sensed something. He looked around as if to see whether a wild animal was on the outskirts of the flock. It was then that he realized it was not an animal. Something was in the air itself.

In the not-too-distant hills, the night sky over the mountains had begun to illuminate as if dawn was approaching. It was unusual. It was the middle of the night. The light was softer than a sunrise. Looking toward the hills, he thought, was something happening in a nearby village? Were the celebrations continuing well into the night this night? The young boy's mind pondered these things, trying to make some sense of what he was seeing.

But the light continued to grow—a soft white light that was beginning to spread beyond the distant horizons. David found it difficult to catch his breath. Without looking down, he touched his hand to his brother's shoulder, gently rousing Jonathan from sleep.

The boy slowly wiped his eyes and tried to focus on what *he* was seeing. He stood and joined David in observing the distant hills, glancing overhead as well to try to understand what he was really seeing. Were their eyes playing tricks on them? Was it that star? Neither boy spoke.

Binyamin and Asher walked over slowly to the awakened boys, speaking not a word, warmed by the fires they—unawares—stood barely steps away from. After several moments, David broke the silence:

"What doeths thith mean?" the child asked.

By now, the light was lighting up the entire valley, even out to the town itself. The barley fields glistened gold as if bathed in the warm misty light of day, shimmering as if in the morning dew or just after a soft rain. The shepherd's hearts were pounding with a gentle nervousness. They were neither afraid nor anxious.

In the town nearby, people were also observing the light, beginning to emerge from their houses. They looked at each other from the streets and windows without speaking a word. From the city's vantage point they could see the light illuminating the hills, slowly moving toward them. Some seemed to be at once apprehensive, growing afraid.

A frightened woman exclaimed that the world was ending, which in turn caused not a small number of people to stir and become afraid. Some went back hastily into their homes, closing their doors shut in fear.

Zechariah's family, having arrived earlier the day before, emerged to see the light begin to illuminate the roofs and streets of Bethlehem. A strange dawn, they supposed. But it was the middle of the night! It was as if the distant hills had awakened the dawn.

Zechariah took several steps out beyond his house, all the while gazing up at the brightened sky. As the light grew brighter and brighter, it became as bright as day. A calm stillness fell over the entire town.

"What *is* this?" Asher spoke, looking up, ignoring the fire beneath him. The light now seemed laid out like a carpet of light in front of them; it seemed to beckon to the distant fields as if the light were alive, as if to point those looking on to what was happening beyond them.

It was as if the light were alive.

The midnight illumination was as bright as the brightest weaver's cloth—even more—white, almost translucent in appearance. Everyone in the fields and in the town *felt* the light. The light gave off a perfect peace that filled them at the same time with awe, wonderment, and calmness.

The star was directly overhead, itself casting a celestial crown that was unmistakable. Something wonderful was happening.

All at once, the light began to move! It began to burst forth as if hitting pools of near translucent water high up in the heavens, the beautiful blue color of lapis lazuli.

The rays of light seemed wrapped in a greater cloak of brilliantly cool light as they descended into the valley, fields, and hillside crevices, where just moments before the shepherds had watched their flocks in a darkened night.

The sky was as bright as the moon would illuminate it on a clear night, but in the most brilliant white, as if born of a more celestial sunrise.

Jonathan, still standing near his brother, remarked: "Look how bright it is." The awakening of light had gone on for just several minutes, though it felt much longer.

Then, slowly, from the heavens there began to be heard by all the shepherds the sound of still, small, sweet voices in the air, quietly speaking, almost imperceptibly at first:

*"Hark... hark... Hosanna... hosanna... Gloria... glory... Glory to God... Gloria... Glory to God in the highest... Glory!"*

Human voices were singing, in the most beautiful celestial sounds anyone had ever heard.

The shepherds stood there with their mouths agape. They saw no one. The voices were unmistakable. The celestial choir grew louder and louder, until the sounds began to cascade down the hillsides right toward them before gently rising back up to the heavens. It was rapturous. The sounds echoed all around the hills and then slowly dissipated.

The townspeople of Bethlehem heard this as well. They could hear the singing swell and echo throughout the distant hills, but heard the *glorias* as if right there in town. The singing filled the air. The people stood amazed at what was happening, swelling with an indwelling they could hardly contain.

Many cried uncontrollably. Many laughed, overjoyed. *"Gloria… Gloria! Glory… Gloria…"* The voices continued.

The sounds of singing were the most beautiful sounds anyone would ever hear. The echo continued to descend down from the heavens right to where they stood and then cascade back up in a sweep of sound and echo. It billowed throughout the hills before resuming all over again.[21]

The exaltations were at times so synchronous that it appeared they were all happening at the same time, yet swarming around them, in the hills and throughout the fields. A celestial display of unprecedented, audible joy.

All at once, and without forewarning, a brilliant angel of the Lord appeared before the shepherds, appearing as one with the clouds above.

They saw him appear first in the heavens and then descend quickly, until he appeared suspended between heaven and earth, immediately above where the shepherds were gathered. His glory was remarkable.

The shepherds, all of whom had been awakened at this point, stood looking at him, unable to take their eyes off of him. At first, they were very afraid and fell to their knees in absolute fear. The angel was all in white. His glistening robe seemed to pulsate as if it itself was alive.

The angel had the appearance of a young man, beautiful, with flowing, golden-colored hair that fell well below his shoulders. He was surrounded by the whitest, brightest light around him and behind him, though glistening blue and white skies or space could be seen in the distance behind him, seemingly extending into heaven itself.

The angel stretched out his hands slowly, extending them beyond the hem of his robe so as to reveal his hands and arms. He exclaimed directly to them:

*"Fear not, children. For God is visiting His people."*

David slowly looked up from among a group of sheep. At the sight of the angel, he had jumped in between the sheep to hide, completely forgetting his crutches. At these first words, and perhaps with a bit of childlike curiosity, he was now unafraid.

*"Do not be afraid, for I am Gabriel,"* the angel continued. *"I bring you good news of great joy which will be for*

*all the people. For today, in the City of David, a Savior is born to you. He is Christ the Lord."*[22]

The shepherds stood utterly astounded. One by one, they arose. No longer afraid, they began to look at each other, and then to the angel. Mouths open, they began to cry. Their tears were joyous. Uncontrollable.

"Why us, Lord?" they each wondered aloud. They had never felt this way before. Not in their hard and hopeless lives. After all, weren't they all just shepherds? Who was this, and why was God choosing them to reveal this great and promised heralding?

David began to clap, standing without the aid of his crutches, now leaning them against his sides. Then, to the shepherds' astonishment, he began to dance! To dance! Without even a sense of what he was doing, he had let his crutches drop at his sides. The young boy danced with utter elation!

The older shepherds just stood there in wonderment, trying to understand what was happening to them, what this extraordinary voice was saying, and what—how—David was dancing!

*"God has fulfilled His promise, made long ago, from of old. The Ancient of Days is visiting His people,"* the angel continued, now virtually within their midst. He was dazzling; the shepherds simply stood in amazement and tried to catch their breath, their eyes never leaving the angel.

As if waiting for them to catch their breath, he continued:

*"And this will be a sign unto you; You will find a babe wrapped in swaddling clothes and lying in a manger."[23]*

At once, the heavens exploded and opened up. The sky was filled with thousands of wondrous angels, all in white. They covered every bit of the night sky in the most majestic display heaven had ever brought to earth. Not since the flood and the bow God had placed in the sky had such a display been given to men in the heavens.

Some of the shepherds said they felt they could glimpse into heaven itself. It was if the canvas of the sky was created for this singular event. The multitude of this heavenly host now began to sing in unison, now visible:

*"Gloria... Gloria... Glory to God in the highest... Peace to all men on whom God's favor rests."[24]*

The shepherds were filled with an incredible peace and joy, jumping, or simply standing and praising God. They began to dance.

This went on for several minutes. No one wanted it to end, this harkening of an angelic choir, appearing in the clearest sky of all, illuminated by the star which had been seen as if coming together for days. The star was the only light other than the angels lighting the sky, piercing it as it was.

"The Lord of heaven has chosen the least among the people—us shepherds—to reveal His King," Binyamin exclaimed. "Praise be to the Lord our God!"

Ironically, it was to the shepherds alone that the angel and the multitude appeared. The people in the town could see the wondrous light pulsating over the hills and the fields. They stood illuminated by this light in the darkened night. The star stood majestically right above the town, as if pointing to Bethlehem. They could hear the voices proclaiming, "*Gloria… Gloria…*" and the strains of an unseen celestial choir coming down to them from the heavens.

Yet the angels appeared only to the shepherds.

Zechariah began to clap and dance uncontrollably in the midst of the people.

"*Arise, shine; for your light has come! And the glory of the Lord is risen upon you. Oh, that You, Lord, would rend the heavens! That You would come down! That the mountains might shake at Your presence.*"

"*Behold, the darkness shall cover the earth, and deep darkness the people; but the Lord will arise over you. And His glory will be seen upon you. Lift your eyes all around and see! They all gather together; they come to you! You will see and become radiant!*"

Recognizing these events as the heralding of God's delivery, he began to sing out in an even louder voice the words of the prophets:

*"The people who live in darkness have seen a great
light,"* he exclaimed. *"God is coming to fulfill the
promises made to our father Abraham and told to
us by our prophets."*[25]

*"Unto us a Son is given. He will rule the nations in
righteousness. He has broken the yoke of bondage just
as He has promised."*[26]

A small group of soldiers stood at a distance of about
twenty or thirty feet away. Two of them—the ones regis-
tering Bethlehem's visitors at the gate a day earlier—then
fell to their knees, silent. They were very afraid.

Zechariah, observing the soldiers kneeling prostrate,
continued with great joy:

*"He will set up His kingdom—a new kingdom, wherein
will reign righteousness. And of this kingdom, there will be
no end. It has been promised to our father David. It will
be as the Lord has promised."*

*"Though the nations rage, His way will be the way
of peace—everlasting peace. House of David, it is a
small thing for the Lord. He is here among you. And
great will be His name!"*[27]

The soldiers were terrified.

In the distant fields, the shepherds stood gazing, affixed to the scene playing out before them. Then, without warning, they witnessed the angels' slow return to heaven and the evening sky's return to deep blue, the star pulsing and seemingly pointing to town. They were overjoyed.

Jonathan had grabbed a ram's horn which the shepherds used to call out to each other. The child began to bang his drum and alternately blow the ram's horn over and over, startling the sheep. In his own way, he was beckoning, announcing what they all had witnessed to the world itself. He was the first to do so.

Binyamin, without giving any thought to the utterance now coming from out of his soul, began to speak aloud the words of the shepherd Psalmist from centuries before.

Hands raised to heaven, he spoke aloud:

*"It is written, Lord: I will not give sleep to my eyes or slumber to my eyelids until I find a place for the Lord, a dwelling place for the Mighty One of Jacob. We HAVE heard about it—here in the fields of Jaar—here in Ephrathah!"*

The townspeople remained standing, silent, paralyzed, bodies shaking with an overflowing of joy they could not contain. Many minutes passed before anyone dared to speak. No one seemed to know whether to stay outside in the now darkened, crisp night, or to return inside.

The star, which many had been observing for days now, was as bright as the sun. It seemed to be right overhead of the city, the light from it piercing a small gathering of pure white clouds. To the people, it almost appeared as if the star was lighting the way into this House of Bread and its humble cave at the outskirts of town.

Zechariah knew Bethlehem was about to visited from on high. The ancient scriptures were coming to life before their very eyes. A night full of light. A choir of angels. A star penetrating the darkness. In their day, in their sight.

Zechariah fell to his knees and then over to his bottom in the dusty road, his hands balancing his limp body from falling to one side. He was out of breath, not able to speak further.

Many stayed in the streets as well. The light slowly returned to that of night, with the star continuing to remain directly over the city. In the fields nearby, several of the shepherds began to gather the flock, which had moved about in the commotion.

The older shepherds said to the others:

*"Let us go to Bethlehem and see this thing that has come to pass, that we have been told by the angel."*[28]

As they assembled and began the short journey into town, Jonathan—drum beating in cadence, and David—walking unaided for the first time in years, led the shepherds across the shimmering fields to Bethlehem, and the newborn Child they believed with certainty awaited them.

# Chapter Twelve
## The Star of Bethlehem

---

The sheep had been bleating and the animals stirring for the better part of the last hour or so. From her straw bed in the rear of the cave, Mary had seen the night become as day. She and Joseph had heard the voices singing and the sounds of the people in the streets. Her spirit was ecstatic. She was completely unafraid.

The entire countryside basked in the glow of golden light. There was a wondrous stillness in the air. In the rustic simplicity of the manger, it appeared heaven itself was ready to deliver its Son. And so was Mary.

Her heart began to beat faster. She could feel her heartbeat increase in her chest and her pulse in her neck, and in her throat as well. She was parched; Joseph, without being asked, brought a gourd of cold water to her and lifted it to her lips, all the while placing his hand behind her head to steady her. She could hardly contain the feeling pulsating through her entire body. She was at the same time numb and ecstatic.

Her breathing increased. She felt all sense of tiredness ebb away, leaving only the strongest desire to sing out in praise to God. All the while, she hardly felt the labor pains that were increasing in frequency and intensity. In a loud, uncharacteristic voice—even amidst the labor—she began to sing praise.

*"Hallelujah, my Lord. You are wonderful, O Lord. Behold, your handmaiden."*

What was playing out here was astounding. Joseph could only observe and marvel, his own spirit filled with ecstasy. Joseph's emotions ran between trying to help Mary and fully experiencing the wonderment that was taking place all around them.

Mary's voice was beautiful, as if continuing the concert of the angels from just minutes before.

*"Thou art steadfast... oh Lord... my God. From generation to generation... You have spoken Your promises... to our fathers... to Your seed forever.*

*"And now... oh God... Only You... Only You, oh Lord... are bringing about the fulfillment of those things... things You have spoken to me... Your servant... yet... the mother of our Lord.*

She continued without pause, Joseph's eyes fixed upon her.

*"You HAVE regarded... the lowly state of me—Your handmaiden—and yet You have done mighty things for me. You are Almighty, dear Lord... And holy is Your name.*

*"Here, Lord... You have put the mighty down from their thrones.*

*"You, oh Lord… are exalting the lowly.*

*"May Your generations call blessed she who bears the Son of the Most High, His Immanuel."*

Mary was filled with the Holy Spirit. No human who ever lived had experienced this. Nor would anyone ever again. Her body was pulsing; tears of joy uncontrollably streamed down her face, washing away any dust or straw flakes that had blown around her in the stable.

Mary's face began to take on a glow from new light, as perhaps Moses' had when he saw God. She was *bringing* His Son into the world.

Joseph contemplated the words she had recalled months earlier, spoken to her by the angel. As Mary quieted down, Joseph came closer to her. As he neared, she briefly fell asleep. Joseph paused and gazed at her, in his own heart asking the God of their fathers to comfort her in this now-imminent delivery.

He prophesied, praying aloud:

*"Your people, Lord, have seen a great light. And now… unto all peoples of the earth… YOU are bringing YOUR bright and morning Star—Your Son… through a daughter of men. Unto US a Child is born; a Son is given… And the government truly will be upon His shoulders."*

Joseph continued aloud:

*"He will govern all peoples and bring salvation to the whole earth. For You have ordained this, Lord, from days long ago—even before the foundation of the world. And*

*these will be Your people, oh Lord. Through eternity, You will gather this people to Yourself as a mother hen gathers her chicks, as an eagle covers its young under its great wings.*

*"You, oh Lord, will shepherd Your people to be with You always. You alone will provide the forgiveness of their sins and bring them back from their captivity."*

He paused for a few moments.

He continued as she slept, unconscious of the birth pangs overcoming her:

*"Throughout every age, what You have brought to pass here this night will be remembered. Indeed, the house of David will never cease to have its King on the throne You have provided. And Your humble servant whom You have allowed to be here will guide Him and keep Him till the day You cause Him to be revealed to all the people.*

*"Glory to Your name, dear Father. And peace to those whom You have chosen to see Him, Your Star."*

Joseph lowered his head for a brief moment.

---

Meanwhile, a few miles away, the revelry of Saturnalia had died down as the night went on. Soldiers and revelers stumbled into their rooms. The streets of Jerusalem became still.

From the palace portico, the King of Judea stood paralyzed, gazing at the incredible star giving light to the southern sky over Judea.

From the distant wilderness, Caspar, Melchior, Balthassar, and their consorts stood in the night, gazing upon the confluence that now appeared to them as a single star in the heavens, as bright as a small sun. It went before them into the lands west of the Dead Sea.

"He is here, among us," Melchior spoke softly. "God has provided a Son to be ruler over all the earth, just as His prophets have recorded from long ago. And we have travelled these many miles to greet Him, and pay Him homage."

Though it was the middle of the night, they were nervous and jittery, anticipation overwhelming them. They gave instructions to their wards to pull up their tents and prepare for the rest of the journey by night.

---

In the stables, as Joseph paused, Mary awoke. The star seemed to direct several beams of heavenly light directly through some clouds that had appeared in the night sky.

The light pierced these clouds and shone directly above the front entrance to the cave, as if lighting the way to its entrance.

Mary began to breathe deeper and lay back on the straw bed Joseph had prepared for her earlier.

"*Jo… seph…*" she breathed out.

She glanced at him and fixed her gaze into his eyes as she began to wince slightly, pushing down with her stomach muscles.

She lifted herself up on her back and gently, modestly pulled the bottom of her garment back over her mid-section toward her breast. She pushed out short breaths from pursed lips, her mouth forming a small circular airway to release them.

Uncertain, Joseph hesitantly moved to the front of Mary. He looked directly into her eyes as he slowly knelt in front of her. She continued her quick breaths, even managing a little smile, uttering a brief sound Joseph perceived as a little laugh of sorts.

He began to cry, and returned quick, joyous laughs and glances to her as well.

As Mary's delivery progressed, a soft, white, beautiful light slowly arose around them, illuminating the entire cave. They could see the animals that just moments ago had been silhouettes against the light of a small lamp Joseph had lit, lying in their places amidst golden straw. One by one, the animals turned toward the light and to Mary and Joseph.

All at once, Joseph could see that they were not alone in the cave. He turned to see two young men, bathed in light, standing on either side of the cave, several feet away from Mary and himself. He was startled a bit at first and caught his breath.

The young men caught Mary's eyes as well. She briefly turned to acknowledge both of them. With this, the men slowly knelt, about six or eight feet from the couple on either side.

The men were clothed in soft white light, their garments as one with their appearance. Each, as in a cadence together, lowered their heads and gazes to the floor of the cave toward Mary. They knelt there, still and reverent—sentries of sorts, accompanying this wondrous event.

In them, both Mary and Joseph unmistakably realized the form of the angels they had met several months before in Nazareth. They were not afraid this time. Their bodies were once again filled with so much of the Spirit that they felt the presence of God, right there in the rustic cave.

Joseph poured water on a large cloth and wiped Mary's brow. Small droplets of moisture were on her forehead. Mary began to hold her breath momentarily and close her eyes. She pushed from her waist and stomach, repeating this several times. Joseph took his place in front of her, gently stroking her legs and caressing her feet.

As Mary labored, she was unaware of any real pain. Her mind drifted off momentarily to her cousin Elizabeth, and her grace in pain. Certainly, Elizabeth must have been scared. She had to feel pain in her older age. Yet, she uttered not an unnatural sound during her delivery or at any time prior.

Mary also thought of Elizabeth's young John, the second cousin of her coming Child; he who was going to prepare the way for her Child. She breathed heavily, slightly panting at the thought of the mission these two young babies were going to undertake one day. It was very real to her. She winced, and a small tear left her eye, coming to rest on her bib. She sighed.

Mary felt discomfort as her Child began to come into view, His little head becoming visible, a head of thin brown hair revealing His coming at the entrance to her womb.

Mary continued to breathe slightly, eyes now open and fixed on Joseph, who was reaching in toward her and her coming Child.

And then, all at once, Mary winced and pushed. The Child slid through her womb and into Joseph's waiting hands, both of which were covered in pieces of clean, white linen cloth he had cut from a garment that Mary's mother Anne had given her.

Immediately, the angels lifted their heads toward the newborn Child. Each raised then lowered two of what appeared as wings from their backs that had not been seen before. The wings folded over their heads, forward, toward and pointing to the Child and His mother, the angels not moving so much as an inch. They knelt to welcome the newborn Child, whom they knew to be the Savior of the world.

Mary, breathing fast and near exhaustion, smiled, all the while looking at her husband, now holding her Child.

Joseph brought the Child to his arms and against his chest, covering the newborn with his own garment to keep Him warm.

The oxen and sheep stood up, and surprisingly, moved slowly toward the Child. The lamb jumped about in the hay. The ox breathed a repeated series of gentle, warm air bursts toward the Child. Joseph smiled and lowered the Child a bit from his breast for the animals to behold. After all, this Child was to be the Lord of *all* creation, he believed wholeheartedly.

It was a solemn moment. An end of their journey of sorts. Yet just the beginning. Joseph, filled with the Holy Spirit, looked up to heaven for a moment, uncontrollably both crying and in ecstasy. He stood up and brought the Child to His mother. He placed Him gently in her arms.

Mary gazed into His wide, now open eyes. They looked deeply into each other for several moments. Mary knew no lingering pain and was at perfect rest as she lay there, sitting up partially in the straw. She slowly spoke a prayer of thanks to her God, with the Child now in her arms:

*"You are faithful, Father. You have brought me to this place and given us this Child, just as You said You would, through Your angels. My firstborn—a Son—just as You have said. You brought Him forth through me, but He belongs now to the world and all that are in it. My heart*

*is overjoyed within me. I am Yours, as He is Yours. Who is like unto our God?"*

Joseph glanced to see the angels still kneeling toward the Child, wings folded toward them, covering their faces. He recognized this posture. He had seen it before. But where? At once, he heard a voice say:

*"I make a new covenant with My people. A covenant of love... of forgiveness of sins. This is the Bread of Life, and the law shall not depart from Him."*

It was then that Joseph realized they were in the same posture as the angels on the cover of the Ark of the Covenant, pointing to each other, covering the vessel. Israel's ancient, visible repository of the Commandments, its law and the evidence of His faithfulness now embodied in this Child.

The law, the manna from the desert—the bread of life—and the staff that would lead all people to God were now embodied in this newborn human Child. The angels paid homage, attending His birth, confirming His kingship over all creation from the moment of His birth.

With this, the angels lifted up and folded their hands in front of them. They continued kneeling uprightly, now facing Him directly.

They remained in their presence, there in the manger, throughout the night.

———

The light of the star piercing the clouds and illuminating the cave had brought many out of their homes in Bethlehem, even in the middle of such a calm, still, silent night. They stood in the streets, curious—some amazed, others looking to each other in shared wonderment.

No small occurrence was happening in their little town, though they dared not venture down the road and fields, believing Mary and Joseph's moment to be private and personal. The entire town, without saying, believed that such an interruption to what was occurring there at the manger stable, they should only view from a distance.

Perhaps in the morning, in the light of day, they would be able to see what had become of this couple, these visitors. But for now, they all slowly returned to their comfort of their homes, their beds, and their children sleeping safely amidst the incredible events taking place mere feet away. The star stood there, directly overhead, they noted. It gave them peace.

Meanwhile, after some time had passed, Joseph stood up and walked over to the side of the cave. He brought over the water and strips of swaddling cloths Tamara and Bilhah had brought earlier in the day. He gently washed the Child as Mary held Him in her arms. Mary then took the strips of cloth and wrapped Him in them.

Once swaddled, Mary took the Child to her breast and gave Him his first feeding. All the while, the Child gazed up into His mother's eyes, she pondering so many things about the Child in her heart, her own gaze un-wavering, fixed on His.

As Mary fed the infant Child, she looked over to Joseph, who was simply gazing at them.

"His name is Jesus," she said to Joseph.

Joseph smiled and nodded in acknowledgement. "He is Immanuel," Joseph added. "God, with us."

He smiled at Mary. She simply smiled and lowered her head and looked again to her Child.

The Child, Jesus, fell asleep at His mother's breast. Joseph picked Him up from His mother and walked over several steps away. He placed Him in the small manger which was there. He had filled the manger with straw and cloths. He gazed at the Child there, in His first crib, and felt a great sense of peace and contentment.

As Joseph moved away from the manger, again, the ox moved over slowly and stood over the Child, his nose barely a foot away from the Child, gently blowing streams of air over Him to warm Him.

As the Baby slept, Mary closed her eyes to sleep as well.

Joseph retreated to a rear corner of the cave and sat, leaning against the stone wall of the cave to rest himself. It was cool.

As morning came, the light of the star still shone bright in the early morning sky. It remained fixed there, even as the sky turned sunrise shades of orange, peach, and blue.

Below, in the stillness of the cave, a new Star had arrived on earth. This one arose in the lowest of places. Born to a woman, amidst the beasts of the field, on a bed of straw, the world welcomed its Savior. The promise made to the fathers so many years ago, now a testament to the faithfulness of God.

For now, Joseph, Mary... and Jesus... slept in the still and warmth of Elimelech's manger. A new day had dawned. God had entered the world.

## Chapter Thirteen
# What Shall I Bring to the Manger?

———

The sleepy little town arose that morning with no small curiosity. Even as the townspeople emerged from their houses, the bright morning sky still revealed the star they had seen, still burning brightly, a small sun in an otherwise clear, azure blue sky.

Zechariah could not sleep that night. Not for anxiety. He lay in his bed, praising God for the things they had heard and seen. He was restless for the coming dawn. He knew Immanuel was in that manger just down the dusty road.

Zechariah did not wait to reach the manger to sing aloud. As he and others walked excitedly together toward the edge of town, his spirit sung out the praises of God:

*"Behold... how good it is when brethren live together in unity. We are all one... we are the children of His promises..."*[29]

His townspeople smiled, and even let out small bursts of laughter—joy—as they walked toward the manger.

They could hear a short, percussive banging, coming from the fields or beyond. Some strained to look for the sound—perhaps a carpenter or stone mason's hammer, echoing across the valley from the distant hills nearby?

It did not take long for people to begin arriving at the cave. The people climbed down the grass hill to the cave's entrance, waiting outside for some word, or perhaps in respect for the woman inside.

There were those who had heard Zechariah's words the night before, anticipating a child that had been born. Then again, some of those felt drawn to the cave, not knowing what they would find there.

Jonathan and the shepherds knew what they would find there.

As the sound of the blunt banging got closer and closer, many at the entrance to the cave turned to see the familiar images of the little shepherd drummer—and his little brother—leading a group of shepherds toward the cave.

"David is walking!" little Atalia exclaimed, in a loud voice.

All turned. From their viewpoint, the townspeople could see the small band approaching—and to their amazement, David, walking without crutches, a huge proud but childish smile on his face, grinning from ear to ear. Atalia and her brother Aman ran toward them, stopping just short of David. They stared at him and his leg, smiling all the while, the star poised directly behind him, framing him and his new posture in full view of everyone.

"Geth who got hith legs back?" the youngest shepherd said, almost inquisitively.

The other two children just stood there, mouths wide open.

"The angels did it for me," the young boy smiled impishly.

Jonathan, in his customary style, bounded ahead to the cave. He moved quickly among the people, pressing under the shed at the mouth of the cave. Without trepidation, the small boy pushed his way through the gathered crowd and then, with only slight hesitation, took two steps into the cave.

Knowing its interior, he looked around. He saw the animals lying peacefully amidst the straw and hay strewn about. There was light in the cave, but mostly an amber, almost dull golden cast throughout it, caused by the slight dust in the air and the sheaves.

And then his eyes caught eyes with Mary.

Mary was sitting up comfortably in the far rear of the cave, still in the spot where she had given birth to Jesus just hours before. The Child was in the manger, and Joseph was picking Him up. He wrapped Him in a clean blue blanket and placed Him in His mother's arms, His Child's head resting gently on her left arm.

Jesus was still in His swaddling cloths, yet also covered in the blanket. The manger now stood as an empty crib, still filled with straw. Joseph was now sitting to Mary's right, a few feet away, gazing with her at their newborn Child—and the young boy at the entrance.

With a mother's simple smile and a slight nod of her head, she beckoned the young boy to enter. In an instant, David had emerged behind his brother, just in time to catch Mary's glance and make her invitation his own.

The two ragged little boys approached the family slowly. They stopped a couple of feet from them as Mary turned the Child toward them and pulled the blanket back slightly, revealing the Baby's face and neck and the swaddling cloths.

They stood in utter childlike amazement without making a sound, unable to take their eyes off the Child.

The Baby looked right at them, making eye contact as if acknowledging them. They couldn't move.

Their eyes opened wide, all at once realizing that this was just as the angels had told them it would be.

Then, they began to breathe faster and heavier. Tears ran down their dusty, ruddy little cheeks. Mary beckoned them closer and raised the Child slightly toward them. Each went to his knees, and first touching the Baby's blanket, shyly looked at Mary before asking, then kissing the Child.

"I don't have anything to give Him," Jonathan said.

Mary smiled lovingly at the young boy: "You have brought your heart," and turning to David, she said, "and you have brought your faith."

The two young boys were the first to see the Christ Child.

In time, a few others would venture inside the cave to gaze upon Him, including Binyamin, carrying a newly-born lamb across his shoulders. He bowed down on one knee to them in homage, all the while with his eyes fixed on Him. Then, he immediately exited the cave.

Another of the shepherds who entered behind Binyamin, having glimpsed the Child, walked back out to the cave's entrance and blew his ram's horn. In one long bellow, the sound echoing across the fields and to the distant hills, he announced to those nearby the confirmation of those things now most certainly known to all.

To ease the stirring of the people outside the cave, Joseph took the Baby in his arms and walked slowly toward the cave's entrance. He went outside the cave to where no small crowd had gathered, awaiting to see the Child. Zechariah continued to tell everyone that God's Messiah was here—in their own midst.

Strangely, none of the soldiers in Bethlehem made even the slightest attempt to see what the commotion was all about, despite having witnessed the events of the night before. They sat in the dust at the city gate, alone.

Zechariah and Esther had stood outside the cave with the townspeople for quite some time. When Joseph emerged with the Child, they moved forward to see the Child. Joseph turned the Child toward Zechariah, whose eyes were drawn to the Child's.

Zechariah bowed his head and walked a few steps away. He began to prophesy praise—the *Shema* to our God:

*"Hear, O Israel: The Lord Incarnate is in our midst! The Lord our God, the Lord is one!"*[30]

Turning amidst the people, he continued:

*"You shall love the Lord your God with all your heart, with all your soul, and with all your strength. These words shall be in your heart. Teach them to your children. Bind them on your eyes, and on the doorposts of your house."*[31]

As Zechariah continued, Miriam and Esther, along with Tamara and Bilhah, entered the cave and went directly to Mary.

"How are you, sister?" one of them asked Mary.

Mary smiled and said, "I am well."

The ladies proceeded to attend to Mary, cleaning up the wet and bloodied cloths still lying near her. With fresh, warm water they had prepared that morning, they helped to wipe her clean and washed her hair. They offered her some sweet barley and bread with fresh water, which she accepted thankfully.

"We've brought some meat and breads for Joseph," Miriam said. "Some fruit and juice as well. I will leave it here for him."

The ladies sat with Mary for a time. Joseph returned with the Child, who was now asleep. Tamara and Bilhah arose and reached for the Child. Joseph handed Him to them. They laid Him back in the manger and opened the blanket. They began to remove the swaddling cloths around Him.

With the warm water and clean cloths, they cleaned up and bathed the newborn. Then, they put fresh cloths on Him. They returned the blanket to Him. They turned the sleeping Child to his side and placed a rolled-up towel behind him. The Child peacefully drifted back off to sleep.

With this, Joseph thanked them for their care and hospitality.

"Naomi has rooms being vacated today, if you wish," Bilhah offered.

Miriam also told Joseph, "Jacob and Johannes and their families will be leaving in a day or so." Joseph thanked them again for their kindness.

Mary smiled.

As the ladies exited, they could hear the quiet sound of someone singing outside the cave. It was Rachel. She was singing ever so quietly, sitting patiently on a large stone. She made eye contact with the women as they came out of the cave and then smiled.

"*Ra… chel…!*" Esther directed toward her, amazed. She could see Rachel's beautiful brown eyes, shining in the midday light.

Rachel rose up and walked directly toward them.

"*Last night…*" she said… "*When the angels sang, I beheld God's heavenly light. This Child will cover many with His healing wings, as He has me. Praise be to the Lord,*" she exclaimed.

The ladies stood there in wonderment, tears running down their faces, embracing. They turned again to the inside of the cave to find Mary and Joseph smiling at them, the Child sleeping peacefully in His manger.

Rachel's eyes, fixed straight ahead into the cave, seemed to both thank Mary and Joseph, and yet, from the depths of her soul, ask what she could bring to this Child whose coming had brought her her sight.

Mary would simply smile with gentle, loving eyes, acknowledging Rachel's miracle. Rachel would give thanks to God through her voice and song for the rest of her life.

———

As the morning became early afternoon, the people dispersed and returned, some to their homes, some to their work. There was no small stir among the people, whose lives had been interrupted by these divinely-delivered events.

The shepherds returned to the fields, praising God for the things they had seen, which were just as the angels had foretold to them.

Mostly, they gave thanks to God for the healing given to their young David.

The shepherds were the first to spread the word about this Child widely, excitedly telling everyone they met over the next several days and beyond about the events that had unfolded there.

Jonathan and David became the Lord's heralds, joyfully telling all they encountered of their visit from the angels and the wondrous birth in the manger cave that they were firsthand witnesses of. They would honor this witness all their rest of their young lives.

Word spread quickly. In no time at all, word had reached Jerusalem about the Child.

In time, the entire world would know that Israel's long-promised Messiah had come.

## Chapter Fourteen
# King of the Jews

It took the *magupati* many months to travel the nearly one thousand miles through the rugged and barren deserts to Judea. They followed the star they had seen in its rising many months before. It led them to the small country they had earlier expected it would.

Throughout the region, as far as Cyrene and Egypt to the west, Arabia to the south, and Persia to the east, the spice caravans were murmuring the word they had heard on their journeys. *Magupati* were en route to meet a profound King whose coming was being announced in the heavens.

Melchior and his associates could hardly contain the excitement they were feeling with each passing day. They were astounded at the accuracy of their predictions and their readings in the heavens as they followed the star that was leading them. The star twisted and turned ahead of them, always making their way clear. When it stopped or retrograded, they stayed where they were, and when it moved, so did they.

Their epic journey was taking them through the region of Decapolis and Perea, toward the east bank of the Jordan River. There, they crossed over and passed through ancient Jericho on their way westward. As they turned south toward the capital of Jerusalem, the star seemed to go ahead of them and pause in the heavens, straight ahead.

It would be customary for these royal visitors to pay homage to the king of the country they were travelling within. Some had told them Herod was staying at his normal summer palace, the Herodian, at the edge of the Judean Desert. As they neared it, they were informed that this wasn't the case. Herod had travelled to Jerusalem some time earlier and was at the palace.

As they neared from the northeast, they were surprised at the clamor on the outskirts of the city. Soldiers were everywhere. Hundreds of people were travelling the dusty roads, slowly approaching the city. As they neared the hill at Bethany, to their horror they saw dozens of crucified men on crosses, lining the roads into the city.

"Not what I expected," Balthassar said softly, as they made their way toward the gate. It was then that all three realized that their welcome there might be something other than warm.

Herod's palace sat in the center of the walled city near the temple complex. From atop the hill opposite the city, on the hill called the Mount of Olives, the three men and their wards stood amazed at the scale of the temple and the temple complex, though certainly its renown had reached all the ends of the earth for centuries prior since its construction by Solomon. They were aware that the walls had been breached by their invaders centuries after Solomon had built it, and the temple desecrated several times. Herod the Great had reconstructed it just a couple of decades before their arrival.

Their arrival caused no small stir in the palace—indeed, in the whole city. The citizenry was aware of this royal visit, as word spread about.

Nonetheless, the three magi arrived at the entrance to the palace. They dismounted and were tended to by Herod's stable hands. Their camels were watered, and their caravan would be tended to while they visited the king.

"We are here to see the king," Caspar said to the gate-keepers.

He had visited Herod once before and hoped that would bode well for their unannounced arrival. The king's steward at the palace was summoned, asking the three royals the reason for their unannounced visit. Melchior answered him without thinking of the consequences of his inquiry:

*"We have come to find he who is to be born king of the Jews. For we have seen his star in the east, at its rising, and have come to worship him."*[32]

The steward stood startled and did not speak a word. He motioned to one of the attendants and whispered something in his ear. Immediately, the attendant sprinted off toward the king's chamber.

Two temple soldiers and a scribe arrived several moments later. The soldiers were in full military array. Their hands never left the scabbards of their swords.

The scribe, though, was friendly—overly friendly—as the magi would later observe to each other. The magi were suspicious of this greeting, though at the scribe's urging they accompanied him up a stairway to the king's chamber.

The three men were announced as kings into King Herod's chambers. Upon entering, they saw that there was no small gathering of people there. Herod sat slumping in his throne, appearing slightly disinterested, though he did sit up and change his demeanor as the magi entered.

There were many members of what appeared to be Herod's family there, including women and children, all adorned with excessive, glittering headpieces, necklaces, and bracelets, and reclining on well-adorned pillows on the floor. Several scribes were off to the side, seemingly arguing about something. They paused from their discussion as the magi entered.

There were several attendants and servers tending to a long table on which were many types of food, meats, fruits, and pitchers of wine. The magi stood, waiting to enter and be invited to join them. Cushioned chairs and purple velvet seats were hastily brought in and placed on the platform near where Herod sat.

Waiting for all these pre-arrangements to be completed, Herod then arose and spoke:

"My distinguished guests, welcome," he exclaimed, motioning toward the chairs with his arms. "You have journeyed far and long, I surmise."

The three men glanced briefly at each other and walked tepidly toward their chairs.

Herod was an imposing figure, with deep brown, haughty eyes and a smile-less gaze. He gave off an aura of unquestionable threat and authority. Some would say his decadence and inner sickness were palpable. Those who served him did so at constant peril for their safety, his moods and whims often preceding rants and fits of unbridled rage.

Caspar, Balthassar, and Melchior proceeded warily, uncomfortably, for visiting royalty.

"Bring our guests some wine, and some food," their host exclaimed.

Not wanting to insult their host, as it was not his custom to partake of strong drink or wine, Melchior said, "Thank you, your greatness; our journey has indeed been long. I would prefer something cooler, perhaps a cool drink of water or juice."

Herod stared at him for a second and nodded toward his servant.

"Of... course," he said slowly.

Anticipating further conversation about the meaning for their trip, Herod seemed to deflect it right from the start.

"You must stay with us to celebrate Saturnalia," he exclaimed. "The august Augustus has proclaimed a great celebration in his honor," the ruler added, somewhat sarcastically. "Pater Patriae is proud of 'his' peace."

"You must tire of the rebels hindering such peace," Caspar offered, patronizingly. "There are a great many soldiers about. We observed many rebels lining the roads to Jerusalem, great one."

Herod slowly lowered and then raised his head, acknowledging Caspar's comment but not wanting to speak much more about it.

"I hear you are following a star," the tetrarch said to them.

"Not just any star, your highness," Melchior responded. "We have observed a historic confluence in the eastern skies over many months now. I would say, unprecedented...?" he added.

"In what way?" the host inquired, feigning both ignorance and surprise at their story.

"Your highness, we are from many parts of the world outside of your kingdom," Melchior added. "I am Persian; my associate Caspar is from farther east in India, just east of the Sindhu. Balthassar hails from Alexandria. We have travelled great distances because of what each of us has seen in our own countries."

"Go on," the ruler answered.

"Highness," Caspar said, "We discern the heavens for our masters. For this, we are paid much and afforded much honor in our countries. As far back as a year or so ago, there were movements in the heavens—unordinary heralds of greatness. At first, we could only track their risings, but soon after we saw stars, heavenly bodies of great light, and constellations coming together unmistakably—to us—playing out word from the Highest to all peoples."

"I first discerned that it was Jupiter rising, highness," Melchior added. "The universal king. Jupiter's journey took it high in the heavens and then retrograded not once, but three times, over a star that stood fixed, as if showing a crown or halo. At first, we thought there might be some connection to Augustus' proclamation of peace—a coronation of sorts, if I may."

Herod grew more and more uncomfortable as these accounts unfolded. Though Herod was appointed by and served at the pleasure of Rome, nonetheless, he and many of his inner circle secretly resented this subjection. Augustus' proclamation only served to inflame their resentment.

"Perhaps this 'king' is in another land?" Herod asked. "Have you considered this?"

"We have, excellency," Melchior continued. "As the risings continued, we saw it heading west of us, perhaps toward Egypt, we thought, or the lands beyond the sea. We started out in haste and simply followed it westward wherever it would lead."

"I was greatly troubled, your highness," Balthassar spoke. "My colleagues were as well. What we were observing has a universality to it, an almost anointing of such a great leader as, perhaps, the world has never seen."

With this, Herod lurched up and flew into a rage. Whatever discretion or temperance he was disguising himself with, his latent and growing fears about a heavenly threat to his throne was more than his insecurities could bear.

"Why here, in Judea?" he demanded. "Don't we have enough kings and omnipotent rulers already?" he said with obvious disgust, directed at Augustus.

"Excellency," Caspar added, hoping to redirect his wrath from them, "we are simply wanderers, are we not? We have come a long way in search of meaning to what we see. We did not—could not—create this."

Several scribes had continued discussing and arguing their differences over these developments since the magi had first arrived in the palace.

"What do you have to say about all this?" the ruler directed at them.

One of the palace scribes, a younger man, a Levite, answered the king: "There are millions of stars, majesty. Who can discern what this one means, or that one says? It is futile for man to try."

Another added: "It would take more than a star to supplant your reign, your highness. A king from these zealots and rebels? Absurd."

The three guests looked among themselves for a moment or two while the palace staff discussed the issue. Caspar raised his eyebrows to Melchior, who, in turn, interjected:

"King Herod, in time, the star redirected itself into a path with Venus. She is the mother star. These two stayed together in the sky almost as one star. It is that which we see in front of us still," he said.

"Forgive me, excellency. There is more. These conjoined stars—the king and the mother—entered into the constellation of Virgo. This 'king' we seek is to be born."

With this, Herod's countenance completely changed.

"Born? *A child...?*" he asked, somewhat surprised, cunningly relieved.

He looked around the room. "I have been wasting my thoughts and restless nights on threats from a *child?*" he yelled. A slight murmur fell over the room. His family stirred.

He called for the scribes and priests who lived nearby to his palace.

"Have them come at once," he demanded.

In very short time, several palace soldiers entered, escorting five men. Word of Herod's turmoil at this royal visit was quickly reaching the streets outside the palace as well. There was no small tumult emerging.

The Romans guarding the streets were becoming aggressive once again, rounding up every person that even looked suspicious. Many were summarily thrown into prisons while the soldiers and the authorities sorted these things out. There was great fear among the Romans of an uprising, which would bode ill for them and the Roman leadership.

"My austere advisors," Herod began mockingly. "Am I not the king of the Jews?" he asked. "Is this not our country?" he continued.

The scribes and Pharisees began to murmur beyond the ears of the temple soldiers, believing their king to be again lashing out at Augustus' self-indulgent decree.

"You are," the chief priest replied, "and it is," he said, hoping to put the king at ease.

He wasn't.

Herod wailed: "Am I to worry about children taking my reign?" he exclaimed loudly.

"What do you mean, excellency?" one of them asked, confused.

"What do our sacred writings say about this?" the king asked. Without gaining an answer yet, he screamed, "Am I to expect a child will take my rule?"

With this, one of the elder priests answered: "We await He who will save us as a people, majesty, as you know. This promise is of old. Many of our prophets have spoken about it."

"Messiah?" he asked. "A child, or a warrior to take my subjects by force?"

"It is written that Messiah will vanquish all our enemies," one of them answered. "In a time of great peril, He from the line of David will deliver the people. It is said that His kingdom will have no end," he continued, seeking to reassure the king.

"But the child?" Herod blurted, unassured.

"Isaias has seen his coming, majesty," the elder continued, unafraid. "It is written: '*Unto us a child is born, a son is given. And the government will be upon his shoulders.*'"

Herod stood remarkably still and coy. In his paranoia, he deduced that this child was not an imminent threat in the least, one he believed he had the power to erase.

"Where will this child come from?" he asked calmly, a sinister smile picked up by the magi drawn across his face.

The scribes declared, "From Bethlehem, excellency. For it is written in the writings of Micah:

*"But you, Bethlehem Ephrathah, though you are the smallest of the princes of Israel, yet, out of you will come He who is destined to rule over Israel."[33]*

"It stands to reason, majesty. The town of David. In his lineage."

At this, those gathered waited for Herod to respond. The magi sat still, realizing they had just heard perhaps their own ultimate destination after so great a journey, now only a few miles away from the palace where they sat.

Herod turned to the three men: "Continue on your journey, my friends. Find me this child, and return word to us, that I may worship him as well."

Abruptly, the king of the Jews dismissed his guests.

He immediately, secretly, began to plan his vengeance on this child, who he thought would be a helpless adversary.

———

It was nearing the end of the day. The three men left hastily. They gathered their belongings and their entourage and travelled a mile or so out of town to make camp for the night. They looked forward to the end of their arduous journey. None of them really knew what to expect at the end.

As they stopped for the night, there it was. The star, still ahead of them, the light guiding these wanderers to what they had journeyed so far to find, their destination now just a few miles away in Bethlehem.

# Chapter Fifteen
## Mary's Heart

---

Unlike the stir in Jerusalem, things were just beginning to return to normal in Bethlehem. The last of the travelers had come and gone from the town. The census takers had returned to the capital, Jerusalem, to bring a full account to the Romans for Augustus' census.

Not a solider was to be found.

Mary and Joseph had taken Miriam's generous offer and moved in with Miriam and Eleazar in town once Jacob, Johannes, and their family had returned to their home in Capernaum. Eleazar and Miriam had prepared their upper bedroom for the little family for what all expected would be a short stay before they and the Child, Jesus, returned to Nazareth.

Mary was glad to return to some sense of normalcy following the months of visions, uncertainty, arduous travel, and giving birth in the cave. The Child was doing well, mostly sleeping and feeding. There was a palpable deepness in His infant eyes that caused visitors to affix their gaze on Him. Many would comment to Mary that He had a special awareness of things from the onset. Mary considered all of these things as she set out the business of raising God's Child.

Joseph spent the time in and around the town, helping wherever he could. He spent a couple days cleaning up and tidying up the cave and manger, even repairing the wooded shed over its entrance, which was leaning from many winters' weathering. He did some light carpentry and masonry work for Eleazar as well. His elderly uncle was glad for the unexpected help.

Mary would often sit outside the house with the Baby in the fresh air. Obviously, the Child was an honored visitor to Bethlehem. The townspeople seemed to enjoy His presence, often stopping by with gifts and supplies the family was grateful to have while visiting, not wanting to be too much of a burden on Eleazar and Miriam. Nonetheless, Miriam and Eleazar loved their company and the opportunity to provide a safe, clean place for them to stay while in Bethlehem.

---

As was the custom in Israel, after several days, Joseph and Mary set out for Jerusalem and for the time of the Child's presentation at the temple. It was a half day's journey from Bethlehem, and fairly uneventful. Upon arrival, they found the city bustling, busy. They made their way in from the city gate onto the small stone streets, passing vendors and purveyors of all kinds of wares.

This bustling capital of the people was yet unaware of the couple and the holy Child right in their midst, including the soldiers, the king, and his royal visitors, though word had been given from the beginning of the census to be on the lookout for what they believed was a zealot Messiah bent on disrupting their peace and rule.

As they neared the temple, there was an unusual crush of people, vendors, merchants, and activity. Outside, in the temple courts, Joseph stopped with Mary at a vendor table selling animals. He purchased two young doves, which he was to offer as a sacrifice and offering in the temple.

They entered the magnificent temple built by King Solomon, rebuilt by Herod the Great. No one could know that this temple would soon be destroyed, this time not by inner strife or an eastern aggressor, but by the Romans themselves in just a few short years.

Inside the temple, the family waited patiently in line, awaiting their designation to a priest. Once directed in, it was here that they presented the Child. The priest in the temple took the Child in his arms and laid him on the show table.

"What name do you give this child?" he asked.

"His name is Jesus," his father answered.

With this simple ceremony, the Child was dedicated to the Lord and circumcised according to the custom of the peoples and the name given them by the angel.

As the priest blessed young Jesus and handed Him back to His mother, an elderly gentleman immediately approached them, continuously staring intently at Jesus. They turned and smiled at the old admirer, not knowing his interest or intention. Filled with the Spirit, he asked Mary and Joseph if he could hold Jesus. They were not afraid for the Child, and Mary slowly placed Jesus in this older man's arms.

The man trembled a bit unusually, so Joseph moved to his side, just in case the man fell faint or was unsure of himself on his feet. Then, looking up from gazing at the Child, he looked at Mary and Joseph and said:

"I am well along in years, children, yet in my spirit God has told me that I will not depart this life until I have seen the Lord's anointed." Then, turning his gaze upward, he blessed God and said: "Lord, now You can let your servant depart this life in peace. For according to Your word, my eyes have seen Your salvation which You prepared before us—a light of revelation to the Gentiles, and the glory of Your people Israel."

The man looked to Mary and Joseph and introduced himself. "I am Simeon, children."

The man again continued, this time from Isaias, the prophet:

*"Who has believed our report, and to whom has the arm of the Lord been revealed? To us! He shall grow up before Him as a tender plant."*[34]

Simeon blessed each of them, and turning to Mary, told her that the Child would be a cause for the "rising and falling of many in their country." Mary simply smiled, acknowledging what she was increasingly learning about her own divine Child, though just a newborn babe. She continually treasured up so much that so many were offering to her, whether learning of His birth and origins or through real prophetic pronouncement.

She stood stunned at the gentle words spoken next by the elder. "And yes, a sword will pierce your own soul, daughter. But this is necessary, so that the thoughts of many will be revealed."

Before Mary and Joseph could even react to the words, an elderly woman approached them, almost completing the old man's words.

"… But thanks be to the Lord our God. For many will seek this Child and His redemption, both here in Jerusalem and throughout the land."

She raised her hands and gazed as she stood in front of the Child:

*"Bless the Lord, O my soul; and all that is within me, bless His holy name! Bless the Lord, O my soul,*

*and forget not all His benefits: He forgives all your
iniquities, who heals all your diseases.*[35]

"It is written, children," she spoke, this time looking
at Joseph and Mary, yet speaking almost conversationally:

*"All we like sheep have gone astray. The Lord has laid
upon Him the iniquity of us all. Surely, He will
bear our griefs and carry our sorrows. He will be
wounded for our transgressions. He will be bruised
for our iniquities. The chastisement for our peace is
upon Him. And by His stripes, we will be healed.*[36]

Mary and Joseph were becoming accustomed to
hearing the voices of the people who were learning the
real identity of this Child, as God had revealed without
announcement to Simeon and Anna.

Simeon and Anna were so sincere, their eyes joyous as
in the fulfillment of great expectation. Though they spoke
of difficult things that were yet to happen, they did so
with love and the inner realization of themselves seeing
God's promises coming to pass. For them, a lifetime of
prayer and faith—belief—were being fulfilled.

———

The Child's journey would indeed bring great joy in
childrearing to Mary and Joseph. Yet they would never
be able to forget the Child's ultimate purpose in coming

into the world, given to them. These feelings would exist side by side within them all His life.

Simeon and Anna blessed the Child once again, with a slight bow to Him as they backed up and departed.

It was a joyous day nonetheless for Mary and Joseph. They had fulfilled all that was in the laws of Israel pertaining to the dedication of their first-born Son. Joseph brought the two pigeons to the table of sacrifice and offered them to the Lord for the dedication of the Child.

It was early in the afternoon. The family planned to return to Bethlehem for a few more days before returning to Nazareth. So, Joseph gathered their animal and filled a skin with water. Mary once again rode atop the beast—this time, cradling her newborn and newly dedicated Son in her arms.

---

As the family slowly made their way on the dusty road out of Jerusalem, Mary was filled with the Spirit. Her joyous spirit thanked God for His blessing of safe passage on all their travels during the journey. And she contemplated the many voices of a full heart.

As Joseph led them down the hill to their destination, the beautiful golden light reflecting off of the grain in the hills and valleys outside Bethlehem was peaceful and welcoming. In the distance, they could see Binyamin and the shepherds tending to a large flock, moving away toward the distant hills.

As they began to climb the final hill up to the town, Mary hoped for some alone time with Jesus, and with Joseph. They were once again thankful for the upper room Eleazar and Miriam were providing. They longed for some quiet and some rest. And to return home to Nazareth.

# Chapter Sixteen
## Wise Men Shall Seek Him

———

Joseph and Mary awoke the next morning to some unusual clamor and clatter outside in the streets. "Visitors," Eleazar said, standing in the half-opened doorway of the house.

As Joseph made his way to the door, he noticed the light of the star still shining over the town where it had remained, unmoved, for several days since Jesus was born. It shone brightly each night, but no longer moved across the sky as it had for many months. The star stood unusually stationery over the entire town.

Joseph looked down and turned to his right to see several of the townspeople lining the narrow road into town and the square, looking curiously at something ahead of them. As he did, he saw the backs of an entourage of men moving away from him. Some were on horseback, following several camels and pack animals. He noticed from a distance that the lead camels were greatly adorned with elevated platforms, whereon were sitting men of royal appearance. As the camels moved along, he could also see colorful silk coverings and gold roping befitting kings and princes.

With much surprise and curiosity, Zechariah walked toward the visitors. Balthassar was the first to dismount. He turned to greet the priest.

"Greetings, your grace," he directed to Zechariah. "I am Balthassar of Alexandria."

With this, Caspar and Melchior joined them. Balthassar continued: "These are my cohorts, Caspar and Melchior."

The men all bowed their heads in mutual respect and continued to exchange greetings and pleasantries.

"May I inquire as to the reason for your visit here?" Zechariah asked, in himself already knowing the answer. Zechariah was also aware that the men were not of their faith. Many in Israel held diviners and astrologers at a distance, as such practices were detestable and against God's law in Israel. Nonetheless, as the one officially greeting these *magupati*, he offered: "We are honored to receive you."

Melchior was the first to answer him:

"We have come to find Him who is born King of the Jews." He glanced over at the star still shining in the day-time sky. "We have been following His star from its rising in the east and have come to offer our homage to Him."

Caspar added: "Our journey has been long. We have been God's wanderers in great time and distance. Do you know where the Child can be found?"

"Several days ago," Zechariah directed to the men, "the Child was indeed born here—in the smallest of our nation's towns and cities, and in the humblest of settings. The King of kings was born in a stable at the edge of our town," he continued, glancing and pointing over in the direction of the manger cave.

The men seemed confused for a moment. They just looked to each other with anticipation, grateful for being led to this place from so far away. Each was feeling a profound sense of affirmation that their quest was now at its end. But a cave?

"We were all witnesses of heaven's announcement of the Child," Zechariah continued. "All the townspeople saw the great lights in the heavens and heard the voices of His messengers in the air, resounding through the hills. Even the shepherds out in the fields were given this great gift.

"We found the Child and His mother in a shepherds' cave. It was there that God brought His son into the world," Zechariah said with humility.

This was not lost on the magi, who realized that the plan of God was more complex to them than even they could have imagined. Being astrologers, they were accustomed to predicting the timings of events. But they were dumbfounded at the nature of all of this.

Nearly two years had passed since the stars were seen in the initial risings. In a seemingly endless journey of many months, across thousands of miles, the accuracy of the heavenly vision had led them to this place at precisely the time of the coming of the King, just as it had been shown them in the heavens and in the writings from so long ago.

"The Son of God, born in a stable," Caspar said in soft amazement. "The King of all kings on a bed of straw?" A servant king, he now understood.

"Who can know the mind of the Eternal One?" Zechariah added. "Even your being here has been foretold; we have it in our ancient writings." He said with great humility:

> "Kings will come to you. It will not be enough; the Gentiles will come to you. The dromedaries of Midian and Ephah; All those from Sheba shall come. They shall bring gold and incense and they shall proclaim the praises of the Lord. All the flocks of Kedar shall be gathered unto you."[37]

The men stood still, in further astoundment at these words. For these were the words of a people not their own, speaking of them through time and distance.

They were filled with the Spirit and thanked God for allowing them to witness this great coming, for being a part of this great fulfillment for all peoples.

"Come," some of the townspeople who had been witnessing their arrival offered. "We will water your camels and horses. Go and see what you have come to find."

The magi walked back toward their camels as each removed what they intended as gifts to the newborn King.

With this, they turned and walked toward the house they were directed to.

*"And the star which they had seen in the east went directly before them and stood right over the house where the young child was."*[38]

Joseph and Eleazar were still in the doorway. Each of the men humbly greeted the three magi, aware of the extraordinariness of the visit. The three men entered the house and found Mary with the Child, Jesus.

———

Miriam had expected that the magi's visit would end in her home, so she hastily had prepared a sitting area where the magi would meet Mary and the Child. Mary had come down from the upper room and sat facing the door.

One by one, the magi entered. Slowly, reverently, they looked at Mary and Jesus. They saw the Child's mother dressed in a light blue shawl and white undergarment, her head covered, with the cloth draped over her forearms. She held Jesus in her arms. As the men entered, she held the Baby out slightly, as if to present Him to the magi.

As the men entered, Melchior was first. He bowed to mother and Child and walked a few steps to his left. Caspar followed him and walked forward. Balthassar bowed and walked to the right, the three men facing them. Joseph walked slowly toward his wife and Child and stood at their side.

With this, the three men went down to their knees, in homage to a king. They bowed to Him and stayed prostrate for many seconds.

"You honor us," Mary spoke. "We are grateful that you have made such a great journey here."

"We have come to honor heaven's King," Melchior said.

With this, the three men reached behind them to take out the gifts they had brought for the Child. Each held an ornate vessel, gold-plated and expertly crafted by artisans in their own countries.

"I bring gold, my Lord," Caspar spoke to the family. "Gold for the treasury of the King and the wealth of His kingdom." He opened the box and revealed many ingots of pure gold, which he presented to the Child and His mother and placed at His feet.

Mary looked at Joseph and slightly bowed her head, humbled at the great gift Jesus had been given.

Melchior came forward. "I give you frankincense," he said. "The choicest resin in my land, for Your ceremonies, for the incense of Your celebrations as the Chief of all priests."

He too opened a sealed vessel, revealing dozens of hardened resins releasing the most beautiful scent into the room. Mary and Joseph both humbly nodded their appreciation of the great gift.

Balthassar stepped forward and bowed to the Child. "I bring you myrrh, from Alexandria," he said. "I offer this humble gift to You for the healing of the nations, for health and for preservation throughout life and death."

With this, Mary slowly arose. She handed the Child Jesus to Joseph, who in turn stepped toward the three visitors. As he neared, the three men again bowed prostrate to the Child.

Joseph stood there, waiting for them to arise. After such a long time had passed, he humbly implored the three men, "Arise, and behold Him whom you have travelled far to find."

The three men leaned up, staying on their knees in reverence to the Child. The Child seemed to gaze softly, directly at them, as Joseph held Him upright. The Child was wrapped in a clean white homespun wrap. This greeting went on for several minutes.

Caspar broke the silence by adding these words: "The Almighty has fulfilled His promise made to your forefathers long ago. He has ordained it for us, not of your flock, to seek Him, to find Him, and behold Him in His innocence. He will certainly grow in the Lord, and in your teaching. His salvation He brings will be over all peoples."

"May the Lord bless you, Joseph, as you teach your son," Balthassar added. "May God our Father be your protection and your help as you protect and provide for

Him and His mother. Certainly, there will be those who will be offended by Him, even seek His life throughout it. May God's blessings and protection be upon Him and you all."

Balthassar turned to Mary and Joseph:

"We have seen Herod," Balthassar continued, his tone turning a bit more serious. "He is distressed at this Child's coming. The evil one as well. I am confident of this. Be at peace. Their battle is with the Great and Eternal God, whose purposes cannot be thwarted, nor can anyone take Him from God's hand. All will be fulfilled."

At this, all three men bowed toward the Child and in respect to His parents. They spoke not another word, but their visit complete, commenced to walk slowly—backwards—out of the house, bowing as they did, exiting to their waiting camels and wards outside.

There were many from the town standing outside in the street. Bethlehem was not usually visited by camels or by royalty, let alone seers who had travelled such a distance to their little town on an occasion such as had occurred here.

Miriam emerged from around the side of the house and presented several of the wards in the company of the magi with loaves of specially baked wheat and barley bread, with dates and almonds made only for the most special of occasions. Eleazar commented, "For your great journey."

The magi mounted their camels and nodded to some in the gathered crowd. They headed down the dusty road leading to the city gate and out of town. In time, those gathered would slowly disperse and return to their own homes with measured confidence and a sense of normalcy.

After the magi and their company had gathered water from the well at the gate, they left the city. A few stadia later, Melchior stopped at the side of the road and motioned to the others. "We should not discuss what we have seen," he said definitively. "I do not feel we should make any report either, at this time, to anyone."

They rested a bit and refreshed themselves outside the town, having agreed among themselves not to return to Jerusalem. For a brief moment, they looked back and saw Bethlehem across the valley, fields gleaming gold in the late-day sun. No one could fathom the journey they had come on. Still, in some sense, they felt it was only beginning.

With this, the company began their journey back home. After several stadia, they turned to the east. They journeyed between the mountains, undetected, toward the Salt Sea.

Passing Qumran, they turned between Bethabara and Jericho across the Jordan, where they found a palm oasis with a spring. They stayed there and recorded their accounts.

In time, they continued their journey past Philadelphia, and through Perea, travelling at night to avoid being seen in the cities and outskirts, and to travel in the cool of night.

After several more days, the entourage turned north through the Decapolis, still hoping not to be seen. They continued away from the land of their destination and toward their journeys home—north, east, and west, in every direction.

Caspar, Melchior, and Balthassar's journey had been long. These wise men sought—and found—Him whose coming had been announced to them in the heavens. Caspar, Balthassar, and Melchior would wander no more. They would seek this God for the rest of their days.

Their work would, perhaps, change as time passed. None would expect great discernment in the stars in the remainder of their lifetimes anything like what they had seen from the heavens in their journey to meet Jesus.

Privately, each wondered what would become of the Child; how His mission would unfold; how His coming would change the world. Would they see Him again?

One thing was for certain. They were called to be a part of the greatest event mankind would ever experience—in any era, from the beginning of time to the end of the world.

The magi's epic journey was coming to a close. They still had many miles to travel to return home. But mankind's long journey with Jesus was just beginning.

# Chapter Seventeen
## Joseph's Dream

Joseph could not sleep well that night.

No one could expect any normal person to take in the events of the past year without contemplating them over and over. The work of returning his family to Nazareth and beginning the raising of God's Son was ever on his mind—and heart.

Joseph was a good and simple man. He had loved Mary from afar, back in Nazareth, watching her grow to a young woman of age, silently hoping no other man would betroth her. She was still a young woman when he went to Joachim and Anne and asked for her hand. He dreamed of making a good life for them, even starting on building a home for them a year before their marriage was consummated.

Though he didn't express them, he often had doubts as to why God had chosen him for the tasks ahead. To validate and claim a woman with child before they were married? To essentially be a surrogate father to a child not his own—to the very Son of God?

Would he be adequate to know the right from the wrong; to know what to teach the child, and when?

Nothing could prepare a man to face the challenges he faced. And then to reconcile angelic messengers, dangerous journeys, distant kings bringing gifts of great value, after a birth in a stable away from home.

With a star pointing the way to where this would all happen.

As he lay in the bed in the upper room of his Uncle Eleazar's house, eyes wide open, he silently prayed.

In his soul, he was perplexed by the words spoken to him by Balthassar, spoken as gently as one could forewarn someone of danger. Nonetheless, he was not afraid—even of the wrath of a demented king. He remembered the words of Simeon and Anna at the temple. He resolved to protect the Child and Mary, confident of God's help.

He drifted off to a deep sleep as Mary and Jesus lay next to him.

In the middle of the night, behind closed eyes, he sensed a familiar illumination slowly lighting up the room. He awoke to find the angel standing there in the room beside him, the same one who had visited him back in Nazareth.

"Joseph, arise. Take the Child and His mother and flee at once to Egypt," the angel simply stated. *Egypt?* Joseph thought in his mind.

"Yes; you will stay there until I bring you word it is safe to return," the angel continued. "Herod is going to try to destroy the Child, and a great many others with Him."

Joseph sat, horrified.

The angel went away as quickly as he came. Joseph sat up, sensing the urgency brought to him. Without hesitating, he arose and began to gather their things, including the gifts they had been given by the magi and the blankets and supplies given to them by the towns-people for the Child.

Mary awoke. "Is everything all right, Joseph?" she asked.

He replied. "I was going to wake you once I packed the animal."

She sat up.

"Mary, a few minutes ago, the angel was here, the same one who visited me in Nazareth. He told me Herod's terrible wrath is about to be visited on the children. He told me to take you and Jesus and flee immediately, to Egypt."

"What children, Joseph?" Mary asked, horrified.

"Many children, Mary. He is looking for Jesus," Joseph whispered, a faint loss of breath coming over him.

Miriam appeared suddenly at the door. She didn't say anything at first but sensed something was wrong.

"In a dream, Miriam," Joseph said to her, "an angel came to me and told me Herod is going to seek our Child, to destroy Him."

She stood, mouth agape, terrified at what Joseph had just told her.

Mary arose, drew a long breath, and picked up the still sleeping Child. Joseph gathered His bed cloths and blankets. Mary quickly put on her clothes.

Miriam went down and woke Eleazar and told him the family was leaving. She hastened to the hearth table and hastily put some bread, cheese, and dates in a sack. Within a few minutes, the families were exchanging their goodbyes.

"How can we ever thank you?" Joseph said to them.

Miriam simply smiled; her eyes, though, betrayed her real concern for them—and for others.

Eleazar came forward and said: "Miriam, I must tell Zechariah and the others. I am afraid there will be great danger here."

Joseph replied, "Of course, Eleazar. Thank you." The two men stepped toward each other and embraced, their arms joining at the elbow.

"We will get word to your families in Nazareth, Joseph. May God be with you," the elder offered assuredly, a slight smile across his lips, yet a distracted concern in his eyes..

Eleazar walked hastily down the side street, as Joseph put Mary and Jesus on the donkey and proceeded to leave Bethlehem. Almost as if sensing impending danger, a dog or two could be heard barking as the lamps inside several houses were becoming lit. It was still several hours before dawn.

Joseph paused for a moment at the city gate to fill two skins at the well. As he loaded them on the donkey's back, he looked back at Bethlehem, hoping against hope that the town would be spared the carnage he was imagining. It would not.

Joseph, Mary, and the Child made their way down the same small dirt road they had travelled to arrive in the town only a short time before. He knew it would only be several days' journey southwest to the wilderness and then on to Egypt. So, once a short distance from the town, he chose a path away from the city and deeper into western Judea to get them there.

As they rode away from the city, in the distance, several hundred yards away, they caught the silhouettes of two small people in the moonlit fields. Despite the distance, they recognized Jonathan and David, watching them leave, a small flock at their side.

David raised his staff in an almost triumphant farewell gesture to them. The family paused in the road.

As the family turned to continue to the road ahead, they began to faintly hear a percussive, repetitive sound. It was the sound of Jonathan's drum, beating out a march to the travelers, as if to help push them on their way.

The drumbeat grew fainter and fainter until at last, the night air was still and quieted. The family was on its way. They would see Bethlehem no more.

# Chapter Eighteen
## Out of Egypt

As the day came to a close, the silhouette of solitary travelers matted against a brilliant orange and pink sunset brought a strange serenity to the family's flight from Judea. Through hills and fields of high grain, Joseph led the donkey that carried Mary and her infant Son.

At first, the family felt an urgency to get away from the capital, Jerusalem. They traveled with haste through Hebron without detection. Perhaps, just any other family returning from what would have been an elongated stay in an ancestral home.

For many miles, the family travelled alone. Occasionally, they would be joined on the road by travelers heading south to Beersheba in Idumea, or points further south and west. Joseph and Mary travelled all day in daylight for the first several days, before finding a comfortable area just off the roads to rest for the night.

They covered seventy-five or eighty miles in the first week of their journey, stopping at roadside stands to buy some bread or dried fish, some fruit, dates, and figs, and to fill their skins with water at the occasional well they encountered. At the end of the first week, they had reached the edge of the wilderness—the same wilderness Moses and the Israelites had journeyed through on their forty-year exodus to Canaan some 1,400 years before.

Arabah was not as hospitable as the more habitable areas just outside Bethlehem and Jerusalem. An occasional company of Roman soldiers would gallop past them without stopping. Joseph shuddered at what might be happening each time he saw the Romans. He could see the same thoughts on Mary's face as they passed. Mary would simply hold Jesus tighter and closer to her as soldiers passed.

A week or so had passed before Joseph and Mary even spoke of the journey they found themselves on, and the perils that most assuredly had befallen Bethlehem's children. There was no word as yet from any travelers. Joseph and his family continued their westward trek with deliberate haste.

"The stars, Joseph," Mary observed one night, once they had settled down for the evening.

As she looked up, she again felt an inward sense of this simple couple's role in a slowly unfolding, eternal drama. Jesus was a "good baby," as people often say. He tolerated His mother's milk well; had a good disposition; slept well; and even appeared to be aware—observing— at times. Joseph and Mary would simply smile to each other when they observed Him looking around and to the distant horizons.

With each morning, the couple felt safer and safer for themselves, yet praying for the children of Bethlehem as they traveled.

It was in Arabah, to the west, that they first heard about the massacre.

As night fell, in the distance they saw a large caravan of spice traders and another smaller caravan, making their way through the hot desert floor in different directions to one of the rare oases en route. Joseph sensed it would be a good location and that they should join the travelers at the oasis.

Joseph pitched their modest covering a few yards away from the caravan's encampment without encroaching on the travelers. He gathered some available wood at the edge of the camp and built a fire. Mary lay down with Jesus. Joseph grabbed the two skins and proceeded over to one of the springs at the edge of the oasis.

As he neared, he began to hear an account from one of the traders to another.

"... An entire company of soldiers—ruthless," one them recounted. "The wailing could be heard for some distance. We heard it. They slaughtered and then just left. Children in their mothers' arms," they exclaimed, trying to understand.

Without a question asked, Joseph filled the skins with the cool water and gathered a few dates from the palms that had fallen to the ground. He went back to his family and found both of them asleep.

Joseph didn't sleep much that night—his helpless mind unrelentingly picturing the slaughter of these children, his heart and spirit feeling the utter grief of the mothers of Bethlehem they had come to know. He pondered whether the men had perished in defense of their children. He was certain many had.

In the morning, one of the travelers slowly made his way toward the family as Joseph was readying to depart.

"Are you Judean?" he asked.

"Yes, by ancestry," Joseph responded, continuing his work.

"We are travelling to Succoth," the man added. "Would you and your family care to travel with us? You will be safer in numbers."

"We are headed to Goshen," Joseph replied. "Thank you; we will go part of the way with you."

With this, the man glanced over to Mary and the young Jesus. He looked to Joseph, yet did not speak, privately wondering if Joseph, Mary, and the Child were fleeing this massacre, and wondering how they had escaped it.

Word had spread about that Herod was wroth with the visiting kings who he believed had deceived him. He directed his wrath to the children of Bethlehem and the surrounding areas. And given the time of the magi's first observance of the star, he deduced that it could have been over a year and a half to two years prior to what would have been the birth of the so-called Messiah who would take his throne.

Herod had ordered the extinction of all children under two. Here, in front of the traveler, was just such a child.

For several days the family traveled behind the caravan, stopping with them to rest at night, never discussing or revealing where they had come from, or Jesus' true identity.

And so, after a couple of weeks' journey, the family arrived in Goshen. Egypt would become their home for some time. Joseph would find work to pay for the small home he rented for the family. They felt safe there. And Jesus grew.

---

One day some time later, another caravan arrived, along with several men on horseback. There was no small stir in the town Joseph and his family had settled in, so Joseph went into the town center to see what was happening.

"Herod is dead," they heard as the townspeople gathered. Joseph didn't care to hear how, or when this man had met his end. He quickly returned to his family with the news, uncertain of his next move for his family.

That very night, as Joseph bedded down for the night, Joseph was yet again visited by the angel from Nazareth and Bethlehem. Once again, Joseph received instruction from the angel, who simply directed him to:

*"Arise, take the child and His mother and return to the land of Israel, for those who sought the child are dead."*[39]

Joseph and Mary arose early the next day. They packed the meager belongings they had and loaded them on a second animal Joseph had purchased to aid in his trade. They said goodbye to several of the people whom they had met and befriended while in Goshen. They left immediately in the morning and began the journey back to their country.

This time, only several miles along in their journey, Joseph was unsettled while they travelled.

"What is it, Joseph?" Mary asked.

"Something is unsettled within me, Mary," he replied. "I have asked God in prayer to confirm where He wants us to go. I cannot be sure what Archaleus' intentions will be toward Jesus, and if he will continue to seek the Child as his father did."

They made their way toward their country, assured by faith, confident of God's protection. Somewhere along the route, several days later, both Joseph and Mary felt a strong sense that they were to return to their home in Nazareth, in Galilee.

Egypt, where God had gathered His people for four hundred years before leading them to the land He had promised them, would once again shelter—this time—His Son. And now, after all this time, it was time for Mary and Joseph to return home to Nazareth, where Jesus would be raised.

Out of Egypt, God was calling His Son. Jesus would soon see Nazareth.

# Chapter Nineteen
## The Journey Home

———

Eleazar had gotten word to Anne and Joachim back in Nazareth that Joseph and Mary had delivered their Child and were heading to Egypt.

All of Israel knew of the atrocities Herod had committed. Many saw these as terrible fulfillments of the words of the prophet:

> *"A voice was heard in Ramah, Rachel weeping for her children because they were no more."*[40]

No one knew for sure what would happen to Joseph, Mary, and their Child. But the family was now on their way back to Israel. Jesus *had* survived the massacre of the innocent children of Bethlehem, and Herod was now dead.

Joseph decided to bypass the route they had travelled to Egypt altogether, avoiding Bethlehem, Jerusalem, and other major centers. Instead, their route home took them north, along the coast, past Gaza and up into Galilee. It again was a journey of many days.

The trip, though long and arduous, was somewhat uneventful. Each night, the brilliant star-studded skies would serve as their canopy. Nightly, it reminded them of the star that had led them, the magi, and many others in the kingdom to Bethlehem.

————

Mary often thought of those they had met—the kindness of Eleazar and Miriam; the faith and leadership of Zechariah and Esther; the wonderful little orphans who had brought themselves to the manger and were the last to see them off.

Mary often pondered the work of the Lord, leading the magi a thousand miles to Jesus to pay homage to her Son. She knew in her heart that her Son would surely save all people one day—not just the Jews, but all peoples, of every faith and nation. God Himself had sent His angels to counsel them and make some sense of these extraordinary events.

The journey gave Mary and Joseph much time to contemplate these things and prepare themselves for what lay ahead. Still, despite all that had transpired for Mary and Joseph, the people back home in Nazareth would have many questions to come.

Joseph regularly contemplated Jesus' birth in the stable. The simplicity of the birth there humbled him. He contemplated all that he had been taught in the ancient writings of Israel relating to the Messiah. Somehow, like many others, he had missed the fact that the Messiah would have to suffer to redeem His people. His perspective changed greatly in the year or so prior to their journey home.

He knew that his Child would "bear our grief." He was haunted by the description of the suffering servant whose bones were visible as He was to hang on a tree, given bitter drink to quench his thirst, in His final redemptive work for all mankind.

Mostly, he thought of his own limitations as a simple man from a simple village. Called to raise the Son of God, and Israel's long-awaited Messiah, he deduced that God would give him all the insight and strength to discharge this responsibility. The journey would be a long one. The Child in Mary's arms had brought this epic to pass.

He knew that for this cause, Jesus had come into the world. He often would ponder how he, Joseph, could possibly be the one to teach Jesus—how to build a house, how to speak to people, teach Him the scriptures. Still, knowing Jesus would build a kingdom, his simple instincts were to just teach Jesus what he knew. He could do no more, he thought. He imagined—dreamed—and often saw Jesus' life playing out before him. These thoughts never escaped him.

Some weeks later, many months from the day they had set out from Nazareth, Mary, Joseph, and Jesus made their way up the dusty path back home.

Their homecoming was joyful.

So, they presented their Son to His grandparents. Anne was to play a constant role in the young Child's life. The family stayed with Anne and Joachim as Joseph resumed his long-delayed work on the house he had begun long before their saga began.

The people of Nazareth gradually came around. No one talked much about the extraordinary events surrounding Jesus' birth. To them, he would simply be known as "the carpenter's son."

Nazareth suited the family well. The seasons changed, and once again, the time of harvest was upon them. They toiled with the townspeople to harvest the fruits of the fields. They were indeed glad to be home.

As morning broke over the sleepy little village, Mary came out to wish Gamaliel and Luke well on their journey back to Jerusalem.

"I hope I didn't bore you with too many details," she said to the men.

They stood speechless for a moment. Luke closed his book of notes and said to Mary:

"Many will attempt to record these things, Mary. I believe I can write an orderly account of this for everyone."

Mary simply smiled.

Gamaliel asked her, almost childlike: "Would it be okay if we checked in on you and Jesus from time to time?"

As he asked, a small child emerged from the house, walking several steps ahead of an older woman. The two men turned, surprised and somewhat nervously, toward the boy.

"This is Jesus," Mary smiled and said to them, "and my mother Anne."

Respectfully acknowledging the older woman, they couldn't keep their eyes off the Child.

Jesus stood there at His mother's side, looking straight ahead at the men, His face leaning on her leg for several minutes. He was a beautiful Child, yet also so normal in every way.

The men seemed unable to find words to speak to Him or His mother. They simply smiled and met eyes with the Child, until Luke knelt down in front of the Child.

"Can I give you something?" he asked the Child. He took out a wooden figurine—a small sheep he had carved out of a piece of olive wood on the journey there—and handed it to the Child.

"You have to be a good shepherd to him, okay?" Luke asked. Jesus looked down at the figurine and then back up at Luke, and smiled at him.

Gamaliel did his best to mask his utter astoundment at seeing the Child. His lip twittered as he drew a long breath and placed his hand on the Child's head. Jesus turned and ran slowly back to the garden in front of the house, his grandmother following closely behind him.

———

Gamaliel and Luke said goodbye and walked over to their carriage. They soon left for their journey back to Jerusalem.

Mary, Joseph, and Anne watched as their carriage disappeared around the bend and down the hill. As they lost sight of the visitors, they looked to see Jesus leading His little sheep in the garden's dirt. They simply returned to their work.

Mary rolled up her sleeves and sat down to grind some meal in the mortar.

Joseph picked up his tools and continued the day's work of building their home.

Anne pruned a fig bush in the garden.

Joseph's mind, as always, was preoccupied with dreams of his Son. He was quietly filled with joy this day as he remembered the words of Isaiah and thought of Jesus:

> *"The Lord has anointed Me to preach good tidings to the poor; He has sent Me to heal the brokenhearted, to proclaim liberty to the captives, and the opening of the prison to those who are bound."*

*"And of His Kingdom there will be no end."*[41]

"And I will help you, my Son," Joseph whispered out loud, unaware, catching the attention of the apprentice.

The men resumed their work. In time, later that day, young Jesus came to them, lamb figurine in hand, willing to help His father in his work.

---

In every city and town, as most went about their business, there was not so much as a thought as to what was taking root in Nazareth. By now, most had even forgotten the strange light in the heavens that had occupied them for many, many days before.

But this was no normal Child, and no normal story. Like the star that announced His birth, one day this Child would Himself be called "the Light" and "the Way." The Child of the star was He that would teach the world righteousness and light a path for all nations toward brotherhood. And here His journey was just beginning.

In this quest, many would journey far and wide to help spread this good news of His coming and His message. Many would be persecuted, even martyred, for His name in the years to come, as the children back in Bethlehem had been.

In time, every nation on earth would know this Child's name, while Herod's and Augustus' efforts at immortalization and self-illumination would fail.

The ancient writings of this once obscure nation were once again proven trustworthy, even to the seers and interpreters of the Gentile world outside Canaan.

A stem had *indeed* arisen from the root of Jesse, just as the prophet had foretold. Heaven had delivered its promised Messiah in the most humble and simple way. A King *was* born to reign on David's throne forever over the children of faithful Abraham. Even the sin that forced Adam from the Garden was redeemed. Thousands of years became tied together in truth, and for the ages to come, in the coming of this Child.

This was of the Lord Himself. As if to validate the truth of this Child's arrival, history itself would forever mark time forward from the time of the Child's birth: Anno Domine. The year of the Lord.

———

Luke would return several times in the years to come. He would record the words, the story, and the events that took place during this Child's lifetime, so that generations throughout time would know these people and events to be true and trustworthy.

———

And so, a dusty little town within the hills and fields of Galilee would, for now, be the Christ Child's—the King of heaven's—home. He would grow up here, learn a builder's trade, and grow in His wisdom. One day, He would truly be about "His Father's business," as He would tell Joseph and Mary a few years hence.

For now, the Child was happy to be able to wander over to His earthly father at work, as His mother ground the grain that would be their bread.

His father would indeed teach Him to build a house there in Nazareth—and when His work on earth was complete, a greater one in eternity.

*"In My Father's house there are many mansions. I go there to prepare a place for you. And where I am, there you will be. Where I go you know and the way you know."*[42]

*John 14:2*

# Appendix

1. Isaiah 9:6-7
2. Isaiah 7:14
3. Isaiah 60:6
4. Numbers 24:17
5. Job 9:33, 33:23-24
6. 1 Samuel 25:41; Luke 1:38
7. Isaiah 53:5
8. 1 Samuel 2:1-10; Luke 1:46
9. Luke 1:49-55
10. Luke 1:43
11. Luke 1:44
12. Isaiah 7:14
13. 2 Samuel 7:13
14. Isaiah 9:6
15. Isaiah 9:7
16. 2 Samuel 7:18
17. Matthew 1:20
18. Isaiah 49:10
19. Isaiah 11:1
20. Habakkuk 3:17-18
21. *The Star that Astonished the World,* by Ernest Martin
22. Luke 2:10-11

23. Luke 2:12
24. Luke 2:14
25. Isaiah 9:2
26. Isaiah 9:6
27. 1 Chronicles 17:17
28. Luke 2:15
29. Psalm 133:1
30. Deuteronomy 6:4
31. Deuteronomy 11:13
32. Matthew 2:12
33. Micah 5:2
34. Isaiah 53:2
35. Psalm 103:2
36. Isaiah 53:4-5
37. Isaiah 60:6
38. Matthew 2:9
39. Matthew 2:20
40. Jeremiah 31:15
41. Luke 1:33
42. John 14:2